Ullapool, *[...]* 2006

Voor Viola:

Omdat ik zo veel *[...]* je hond

Far Inland

en omdat ik zo blij ben dat we samen hier zijn!

mooi hè?!

Richard

FAR INLAND

Peter Urpeth

Polygon

First published in
Great Britain in 2006 by
Polygon, an imprint of Birlinn Ltd
West Newington House
10 Newington Road
Edinburgh
EH9 1QS

9 8 7 6 5 4 3 2 1

www.birlinn.co.uk
www.farinland.net

ISBN 10: 1 904598 38 2
ISBN 13: 978 1 904598 38 1

British Library Cataloguing-in-Publication Data
A catalogue record for this book is available on
request from the British Library

The publishers gratefully acknowledge subsidy from

 Scottish
Arts Council
towards the publication of this volume

Typeset by Palimpsest Book Production Limited,
Polmont, Stirlingshire

Printed and bound by
CPD (Wales) Ltd, Ebbw Vale

Dedicated to the memory of Giles Gordon

Tha a smùid fhéin an ceann gach fòid, 's a dhòrainn ceangailte ri gach neach.
Every peat has its own smoke and every person his own sorrow.

Traditional Gaelic proverb from *Folksong and Folklore of South Uist* by Margaret Fay Shaw

'The inhabitants of this island had an ancient custom to sacrifice to a Sea God call'd *Shony* at Hallow-tide, in the following manner: The inhabitants round the island came to the Church of St. *Mulvay*, having each Man his Provision along with him; every Family furnish'd a Peck of Malt, and this was brew'd int Ale; one of their number was pickt out to wade into the Sea up to the middle, and carrying a Cup of Ale in his Hand, standing still in the posture, cry'd out with a loud Voice saying. *Shony, I give you this Cup of Ale, hoping that you'll be so kind as to send us plenty of Sea-ware, for inriching our ground the ensuing year;* and so threw the Cup of Ale into the Sea. This was perform'd in the Night-time.'

From *A Description of the Western Islands of Scotland* by Martin Martin, 1703

Moved

The great sea stirs me.
The great sea sets me adrift,
it sways me like the weed
on a river stone.

The sky's height stirs me.
The strong wind blows through my mind.
It carries me with it,
so I shake with joy.

by Uvavnuk, translated by Tom Lowenstein.

ONE

Sorley MacRath had the gift of *second sight*. If he had always had it, he could now not be certain as his earliest memories were so vague, but as far as he could be sure *the gift* had always been a part of his life. In childhood it loomed in his future life like an Atlantic storm on the horizon; in adulthood its insanity all but devoured him.

As a child he had seen the suffering endured by his grandmother, Morag, who had the same gift and who seemed to be always in a state of great sorrow. He remembered clearly that at times she was hysterical at the visions she saw and she was then confined to her room and was tended to by his mother and other women of the village as she cursed at her bad fortune.

At other times she was reflective and quiet and would sit for hours by the open fire. She had a fondness for telling Sorley the old tales and stories of the family and the village and sometimes of the gift they shared, stories she would tell in a low, soft voice, and while she spoke, her hand, held open and flat, would gently tap a slow steady beat on the wooden arm of the chair.

She told him of the harm the gift of second sight had brought to almost every generation of their people and yet how in every generation the gift seemed to get weaker and its bearers became fewer in number.

She told him that he would be no exception in this suffering, and that was the day he knew he had been born with a sign that the gift was already within him – he was born with a single tooth already grown in his mouth.

Some, Morag told him, held that the tooth foretold of the gift of sight but as many again that it was a sign of the gift of healing, but she knew that he had the gift of sight, and that tooth, whether of sight or healing, never fell with his other childhood teeth and remained in place when his adult teeth came in.

When his grandmother first moved to the family home, Sorley endured the night terrors she suffered; terrors she expressed in anguished mutterings audible throughout the house. Her sleep was feverish and in it she saw a gallery of faces, the departed and troubled souls who meandered through her dreams.

When she wasn't dreaming, Sorley would hear her pray to God for relief from her torments, and if her prayer was not granted then she would plead for the Lord to allow her to die peacefully in her sleep. Sometimes it would seem that her prayers had been answered and the visions would cease for days or weeks or months in which Morag would be peaceful, more youthful and would regain her appetite until, inevitably, they returned to her, coming in waves as though driven by great storms.

Then the storm would pass again and Morag would consider the visions in turn. Some would be confused and beyond her understanding and these she would discuss with other women of the village, searching for their meaning.

Others were clear to her and were terrible in their message, and these she would struggle with and try to suppress and rationalise what they warned was to come.

One dream, one vision, haunted her. In it she saw again and again the face of her husband as she had seen him just days before his death, walking towards her in her dreams, on the darkness of a winter night.

In her vision he was staggering from step to step as though in agony, his clothes hanging in shreds about his weakened frame. As he approached her she saw that there was seaweed in the place of his red hair, and she knew at once that this was an omen, a death foretold, the death of the one closest to her.

A week before she first saw that vision she had pleaded with him not to go out on the sea again, to leave the fishing to the younger men and to remain at home. But he was stubborn and proud and would not listen to what he thought of as the simple rantings of his wife. Within a month he was dead.

He had woken early one morning and had found the day set fair for fishing the reef, maybe ten miles out along the coast. A strengthening southerly wind would, he knew, carry the boat rapidly to the vicinity of those rocks, and so the crew of five local men set out in the wooden boat, *An Sgarbh II*, they had sailed since the days of their youth.

The southerly wind had raised a strong, rolling current that grew such that it turned shoulders of white water under the boat from her stern as she sailed towards the reef, lifting and dipping her. They knew this to be the most dangerous of winds off that coast, but sailed on, keen for a good catch.

The only surviving member of that crew had recounted how they were within sight of the reef and were preparing lines to start fishing for herring, when the swell grew rapidly in advance of a squall and a large wave had lifted the boat and dropped her stern-first into the waves, swamping the open thwarts.

The boat sank rapidly, taking down with her four of the crew. They hadn't a chance no matter how they swam or kicked, but one survived, clinging to a barrel and he was washed ashore.

As night approached on the day the fishermen went to the reef and the boat had not returned to the harbour, the wives and mothers of the crew had gone to the beach expecting to see the boat's red sail peek above the headland and then into full view in the narrow mouth of the harbour. All but one had gone to that shore in hope and expectation, all but Morag, for she knew that the boat would not return, and that the men were lost. She had seen it and knew it to be true. Morag stayed inside the house that night, alone by the fire, numb with sorrow while the village thronged with frantic action as boats set out to search for the missing men and fires were lit on the headlands and by the shore. But their actions were to no avail. Darkness came and with it came realisation and acceptance that the men were lost to the waves.

When news came that a survivor was found, half dead on a distant shore, hope came to their hearts and spread among them like summer fire. At first he had not the strength to speak but finally he told of the wrecking and broke their hearts.

Within a week, reports were received in the village from a settlement further in the north, that bodies had been seen washed onto the inaccessible rocks that ringed the very northern tip of the island. High winds and stormy seas meant that nothing could be done to gather them, and as the southerly wind continued to drift and roll the tide out towards the northern Atlantic, it was accepted that those bodies would never be recovered.

While the bodies never came back, the vision of her husband lying there with seaweed in his hair, the seaweed she had seen in his hair as he walked the roadways in her visions, never left her, and the torment seemed only to grow as no end could be brought to the matter with a burial in the village cemetery by the dunes.

When the sea carried him away from her, it had also compelled him to walk in her imagination and he walked on in perpetuity, a drowned man locked in her night-time terror.

Many in the village considered the visions endured by Morag to be nothing other than fanciful indulgence, but many others had memories of elderly relatives who had also suffered from the same blighting gift, and these folk sympathised with her struggle.

Yet, in their sympathy there was also fear, and when his grandmother had finally come to live with them, most of the younger generation in the village stayed away from the MacRath house and its new resident.

The family became increasingly inward-looking and isolated, and although Sorley's father toiled on the land with the other men of the village, the family were not known to mix with anyone but their own and their close neighbours.

At school one day, Sorley overheard a whispered phrase; the family were *neònach*, they were queer people, and the shame he felt upon hearing those words stayed with him, for on the island, once named is always named.

On the day before she died, Morag asked Sorley if he liked the island life, if he liked the croft and the moors, the sea and the dunes?

He did not answer her and she said to him, 'I see it in your eyes, Sorley, I see the cold light in your eyes, the gift is yours.'

When she died, suddenly and quietly, Sorley ran from the house out onto the moors and stayed in hiding by the river, not returning even at nightfall. His grief at her loss was more powerful than any emotion he had felt before and he ran from the house as though he could run from the sorrow.

He stayed by the river that night and for two days and nights beyond, hearing familiar voices out on the moor calling his name.

As darkness closed on the clear sky that first night, a glow gathered in the north like that of the last hot ember in a hearth, lighting the low, distant sky beyond the hills.

Slowly, flashes of pale green light flew from that ember towards a point high above the village, and the voices of those searching for him out on the moor gave way to the unfamiliar voices that rose with the Northern Lights – the *fir-chlis*. Sorley stood and beckoned the dancers to come to him, encircle him and lift him from the grief of love and death, and they came, taking him towards that ember, towards the flame in the far northern sky.

He did not return home the following day, missing the wake. Eventually he was found, lying close to the riverbank, emaciated with hunger and cold, his hands cut and frozen and clutching river stones.

'Sorley, Sorley,' his father uttered when he found him at the riverside and Sorley thought his words were tender, more tender than any his father had ever said to him. 'Come home, Sorley,' said his father as he lifted the body of the boy in his arms.

Sorley was confined to bed. He knew that his mother's grief at the loss of his grandmother had been compounded by his actions. Sorrow had also turned to shame and whether true or not Sorley felt that his mother never forgave him for running out on them and hiding, nor loved him the same from that day forth.

In the days that followed, it was not the bitter chill of the winter air that he recalled of his time on that moorland but the brilliance of the winter night, the Northern Lights and the starlit darkness. Under the veil of a thousand galaxies he had wandered not on the land but through the skies of the north, searching for his grandmother, and had found her in the flowing of the river, the glowing of the winter night and the grey light of the winter day. He'd heard her in the curlew's call and the crow's caw.

After returning home, Sorley took to sleeping in his grandmother's curtained box bed. At first, the room was a comfort to his sorrows and he resisted his mother's attempts to remove the objects his grandmother had left behind.

Sorley's mother would enter his room at night and look at the sleeping child. She saw how distant he looked when he was dreaming. He did not turn or kick or flail his arms but lay rigid.

Behind his closed eyes, the boy saw the mountains and the jagged edges of a broken summit line revealed to him by a break in the storm clouds.

He was standing close to the summit on the round shoulders of a mountain. The summit, rising from a steep plain, was bound in snow that in the evening light was grey-white and held the last pink of the day at its fringes. The cloud above the mountains was angry. He was terrified, as though he were watching violence from afar; feelings he knew belonged to a place beyond childhood.

The time of this repeated dreaming was short, maybe lasting only for a month or two until Sorley woke one night and got out of the bed. He walked to the window and drew back the curtains. His eyes focused on the darkness of the night and he did not initially see the figure walking from the house.

Then, as his eyes grew accustomed to the dark, he saw the small boy running towards the moors. The boy's running was awkward and he made a slight twist to his body as he moved, as though in pain. His identity was unmistakable; it was Calum, his neighbour.

In the moment he saw him out there, Sorley knew that Calum was running with terror, as though being pursued by someone or something unseen. Sorley began to weep and then, as the running boy disappeared into the darkness, he yelled out, unable to bear the horror.

The bedroom door opened and his mother came in.

'What is the matter, Sorley?' she asked.

'Calum is on the moor, I can see him running,' replied Sorley.

His mother looked out of the window.

'There is no one out there, Sorley, you have been dreaming. Look,' she said, holding back the curtain for Sorley to look again.

Sorley looked out and he saw Calum running.

'There, there he is!' he screamed at his mother, pointing towards the far bend in the road.

'He is not there, Sorley,' his mother insisted. 'Calum is at home with his family. You've been dreaming,' she said, trying to placate him. She closed the curtain and led the sobbing boy back to his bed.

TWO

The attack was as sudden as it was unexpected and its ferocity disarmed its victim. When the breathless beating had stopped, the battered man lay prostrate on the pavement, his eyes watching a small stream of blood running into the gutter from his broken mouth.

Sorley lay in the shadows, unable to move, such that a passer-by might have thought he was dead. The street was empty except for the dark form of his assailant stumbling away, his breath rising into the cold night air in a thin twisting column as he slowly disappeared into the night.

In the attack, the books he was carrying home in an awkward, unbound pile under his arm became scattered about the road, their spines broken and their faded pages soaking up the slushy rain and dirt of the road's tarmac surface. The pile he carried that night was no bigger or smaller than the pile he carried home most nights from the small lock-up he ran as an antiquarian bookshop but one of the books was larger and more awkward than the others, heavy in its leather binding.

A fox came from the dark opening of a nearby close, pointed its nose into the air sniffing out the source of its excitement and ran towards the body lying on the ground. It stopped close to Sorley's face, sniffed again and then licked the blood that ran from the wounds beneath his hair. Sorley did not – could not – move. The fox then nosed and sniffed about among the old, scattered books, lifted its leg over the largest one of them and pissed on the open pages of text.

The fox was then distracted and raised its head into the wind before running back into the darkness of the close and Sorley was alone again on the street and could not fight the heavy downward draw of unconsciousness as his eyes closed and his thoughts left the pain of his wounds until he suddenly felt his body being lifted. In the movement he felt pain from the broken ribs in his chest, and he felt a looseness of blood running freely down through his skull, dripping out through his mouth and nose as he was lifted from the pavement. His mouth hung open as though yelling, but he was silent and a broken tooth – his first tooth – jagged his tongue.

Sorley looked down at the place where the attack had occurred and there on the pavement was his body and his bones were exposed and gleaming and seemed cleaned of their flesh and blood and were white as though they had weathered in the open air for many winters.

He climbed further into the sky and his arms were outstretched. As he flew upwards the pain of his wounds left him. He felt warmth in his body, up there in the low sky, as he flew on his new wings and the scene of the attack and the surrounding streets were gone from view. The amber glow of streetlights also slowly faded and he was in darkness but for the bright white glow of a thousand stars above his head.

The roar of the city traffic had gone and was replaced by the sound of gently lapping waves and the shrieking and piping of sea birds calling from cliffs, close at hand.

He woke at the coast and was lying on the open floor of a small boat. The boat had no oars with which he could move it or guide it in the water, yet he could feel that the boat was moving slowly in and out with the waves as though locked in the force of the current that moved silently in the shallows.

Above him, a small, white gull glided in unison with the boat, and called out in long, piercing shrieks and the ink-black sky was cut with white streaks as stars fell to the ground.

Sorley raised his head above the rim of the boat and saw on the near shoreline an arch of large, weathered whale-bones dug into a haunch of dunes that shouldered a small bay. He could see along the shoreline, silhouetted in the starlight, the curved shapes of other bone arches, maybe twenty or more.

Finally the boat rode its keel into the sands. Sorley climbed out and walked through the breaking waves that ran on and lapped the shore. There, before him, was the largest of the bone arches and before it was the body of a dead animal, a seal.

He crouched over the remains. The seal's fins had been stripped from its sides and in its lower back a deep gash ran brightly with fresh blood. Steam came from the wound and from the weep of blood that trickled onto the damp sand.

Sorley felt a compulsion to touch the fatally wounded animal and bent over the carcass and placed his hand inside the wound. His fingers felt the lustre of the seal's liver and it came away from the gut without effort as he gently pulled at it and brought it out through the open wound into the night air. He raised the warm flesh to the sky and then began to eat its clot of iron that broke easily and melted as if it were butter as he swallowed it.

A small burn broke across the sand and Sorley cupped its water in his hands and poured it into the seal's mouth until its thirst had been quenched and its spirit was free again.

He walked on and from the summit of the dunes he could see starlit moorland stretching out before him and, in the distance, the steep white peaks of snow-covered mountains, visible through the darkness. The seal blood was drying on his hands and on his lips. He rubbed his fingers on the naked skin of his forearm and again he felt his body rising.

He was in the sky once more, facing down and looking back at the oar-less boat, the shore, the bone arches and the seal remains and then, before him, the black moorland.

His arms were outstretched and, still rising, he saw before him that the moorland gave way to snow-covered mountains and beneath their steep contours he could see rolling hills covered in silver-birch forest.

Above the snowline he came to ground, and the rock faces closest to him were overhung with wind-sculptured jags of snow and ice. He walked on towards the highest peaks and then he started to run, bounding through deep drifts. He looked at his body as he moved through the snow. His skin was now white fur, and he ran on his feet and hands.

At a cave close to the summit of the highest peak he was back on his legs and was human again. He walked into the cave and saw the bones of a man lying there, not long dead. The skull, although without flesh, still bore the faint dark red coloration of skin and the mouth was open, as though he died singing. Sorley knew that the bones were his own and he would wait in the cave until they were healed and flesh grew about them.

The glistening blue-gold light of the Arctic night shimmered in the cave and Sorley saw that the bone hands held small, flat stones and in the centre of each stone was a time-worn hole. The hands were open as though offering the stones to him, and Sorley took a stone from the hands and placed it in his mouth and within seconds his mind was drifting from the cave. Before him, emerging from the darkness, he saw a slow gathering of faces. Among them was his grandmother. She was talking, her mouth barely moving but moving in patterns as though reciting some short incantation. The sound of her voice was not audible to him. Her eyes were open. Her mouth shapes were not those of Gaelic or English but of some other tongue.

As he felt the stone on his tongue he heard voices unfurling stories in his head with an immediate and insistent ferocity such that he could not stop himself from mouthing the words as they were spoken to him. Some of the stories he knew from his childhood, others were new to him but all seemed to be bound to him in fact or blood: a legacy, a gift, the history of a gift.

And Sorley reached for another stone.

Second Stone

Darkness is falling on the island.

A woman is walking across open moorland to a secluded bay, ringed by high cliffs. The shape of the bay, its narrow aperture and steep floor, brings a last late force of energy to the curl of the waves that break on its white sands. The echo of those waves rings about the cliffs such that the calling and piping of the sea birds can be only faintly heard above their breaking on the shore.

Fulmars nest on narrow ledges and sea pinks grow from every crack and split in the rock. The face of the cliffs is rounded and undulates as though a thousand boulders were held there, frozen in their fall to the sea.

The woman, in dark clothes, descends the path to the shore and what is lying there. She carries a crude chisel and as she reaches the edge of the shore she picks a large stone from the base of the cliff.

She walks on towards the slumped body of a whale and as she approaches its remains a clutch of oystercatchers take to the wing, calling across the bay as they fly low over the curled white water of the breaking waves. Terns flit and call raucously over the body.

The woman kneels down close to the whale's mouth and places the blunt chisel blade between its teeth. She raises the stone and hammers the chisel into the gums, slowly edging and turning the teeth, cutting the gum and chipping at the blood-drenched sockets in the jawbone as the teeth loosen. She holds and twists the exposed tips of the worked teeth until one comes free in her hands.

She begins again and works until, in total darkness, she has gathered four of the whale's teeth and then she leaves that shore and the body of the whale and returns to her cottage, far out on the moor. She knows that the teeth will harden and that she must work quickly if her wishes are to be fulfilled.

At home she works in the red glow and thick smoke of the peat fire, cutting at the teeth, shaping and marking, gouging each successive ring of growth until each tooth is carved into the form of a whale. She rolls the four whale teeth inside a cloth and waits patiently for their time to come.

Sorley took another stone from the bone hand and another until the hands were empty, and each stone spoke for a day and a night.

The bone hands held the stones as though in some order but Sorley took them as they came, and some fell onto the ice as the hands slowly emptied and their stories were lost.

As he heard the stories and spoke their words he was not speaking but barking, yelling, growling. He whistled and sang like the birds, his feet stamped the ground around the body as he talked in this strange tongue. He clapped his hands. He shook his head like a courting grebe. His skin was fur and feathers then scales and shell. He had a tail and wings, a snout and then a beak, claws and then hands. He crawled on his belly and ran with the legs of a horse. He was man and animal, bird and fish.

An Arctic fox came to the cave mouth and howled with him, their calls binding together in the Arctic air, the Arctic night.

Third Stone

The incessant rain had left the fields sodden and most of what had been planted had rotted away into a crumbling, fibrous mass that would not reward with sustenance the effort of digging it from the ground.

As their fears began to take hold in reality, an air of misery descended on the district of the northern villagers, and it became clear that unless the storms abated many of their number would starve that winter.

Donald knew that he would have to kill the calf, or even the cow and calf, if they were all to survive through to when a more constant supply of fish could be brought from the waters of the Atlantic. As it was, good fishing days had been few and far between that year, and the barrels of salted mackerel and herring were running low at a time when most would have been laying in a good store for the lean months to come.

Donald looked about him at the wretched bareness of the cottage. He saw the pale faces of his wife, Margaret, and son, Angus. He heard their baby screaming from the far room. He looked at them and wondered who would fall first that winter, which one of them he would have to bury first.

They had, like most other families, already devoured the thick, black, salted meat of the solan goose that came from the sea cliffs and remote sea stacks in the late summer. Another boat had left the harbour bound for the island of Sula Sgeir in an attempt to bring another catch back to the district for the winter. But nothing had been heard of its crew in a month, and the seas were now too rough for anyone else to venture to those distant, barren rocks with their sheer sea cliffs to find the missing men.

The village boats, the *sgothan*, had all but dried out on the shore: it had been so long since the menfolk had been able to push their eager prows out into the breaking waves.

Every morning a huddle of anxious men stood silently at the shoreline gazing out into the impenetrable storm. Waves broke on every headland throwing white mist high into the surrounding fields, and every morning one of their number reasoned that the storm would break that day. A few persisted in fiddling and worrying at their fishing gear, cleaning lines, darning the smallest of holes in the boats' large canvas sails, work carried out to try to make it seem that somehow they knew the weather would break very soon, and they would be ready. But no one knew when that day would come.

Margaret had begun to reduce the food she ate so as to feed the children, and she was looking, to her husband, more thin and pale as every day broke the same as the one before, with fierce winds and falling rain, and with an all-pervading sense of dampness and chill entering their bones.

The cottage was growing cold as the high winds quickly drew the usually morose, heavy peat smoke from the main room and out through the reed thatch and it was then that Angus started to cough. Within a week his hacking lungs had brought blood to his mouth, and his frame began to dwindle almost before their eyes. His mother brought him fresh, warm milk every morning, and nearly all they had from the starving cow went into the boy. But every morning he refused to drink it all, and when he did take a mouthful he spluttered it out onto the bedclothes and coughed fiercely with weak, desperate tears of pain running down his bone-white face.

A week on and Donald slaughtered the calf in the byre. His usual hesitance in these matters had all but disappeared as he took the gutting knife from his belt and drew it quickly and deeply across the animal's throat. The beast gave a sudden start as the blade went into the slack throat flesh, and then it stood motionless.

At first, his round, black-moon eyes stared at Donald, and then its gaze wandered as the blood ran down into the basin Margaret had placed on the byre floor. The animal fretted at the restraining rope tied around its back legs, and when it became too weak to stand, Donald hoisted its back feet into the byre roof, and the dying animal hung there motionless with only the sound of dripping blood splashing onto the sides of the pail.

'I should have had the boy with me this year when we went to the well,' said Donald to Margaret in an accusing tone.

'He's too young,' she replied, 'the shock would have killed him.'

'Well, look at him now, is this better? Neither land nor sea has given us anything this year, and I reckon that every other house in this village will have a lad like him before the winter is out.'

The sound of the boy coughing filled the cottage again, and Margaret left the byre and went to him. Donald put down the knife and followed her to the bedroom. Their smallest child, a baby of only six months, wailed from a box crib at the side of the room, but Margaret did not leave her eldest to attend to the crying child.

Donald stood uncomfortably in the doorway. He had lifted the child maybe once or twice since it was born, and then only when his wife was in the field or too far from the house to hear him crying.

'You tend to the baby,' he said to Margaret, 'I'll stay with Angus.'

Donald approached the bed and saw before him a child with an almost deathly grey complexion. The child did not move his eyes to greet him, or utter any sound, as both actions seemed too much effort now for the little life he had left in him.

Father looked at son, and he realised that for all his chastisement of the boy in his weakness and in his almost constant muteness, he was his son, and the death of the son would destroy the father.

The following morning, Angus did not wake. He was unconscious when they went to him first, with only the slightest detectable pulse beating in his thin wrists.

The cottage filled quickly with elderly women, all relatives of Margaret's, and each in turn sat at the bedside. Some prayed, others wiped the boy's brow with warm cloths. Each said the same, a diagnosis delivered in whispers: *A' chaitheamh*. As darkness approached, Donald knew that he had to find some help or the boy would be lost. But he knew, too, that the nearest physician was over two days' walk from the village.

Maybe it was too late. A lay preacher came to the house, and Donald, urged on by his wife, let the young man into the bedroom, and he prayed over the child. As the preacher prayed, one of the women left the cottage and returned shortly after with a small fine-cloth nightshirt, wrapped in a bundle of soft blankets. Donald knew that it was to be Angus's *marbh-phaisg*.

When the preacher had gone, Donald took Margaret to the byre.

'I have to go to her,' he said. 'If she cannot help, at least we will know what is to happen.'

'No, Donald, stay away from her. What good can she bring to us now? She's brought only shame on this house.'

There was no reply from Donald, and Margaret saw that his face was red as he sobbed tearlessly, and she left, unable to watch him cry.

Donald took the knife from his belt again, and went to the hanging calf. Still sobbing, he placed the blade under the fat at its neck and drew it down, opening the skin out from the animal's flesh. Although the calf had been dead for nearly a whole day, steam still came from the gash behind the knife.

When he had removed the skin from the animal's body, he carefully cut in around the head, circling the ears and eyes and the juvenile horns, finishing where the mouth and lips left a cavity.

Donald placed the hide on the byre floor and rolled it, still complete, tucking the legs and head into the roll. Small flecks of raw, red muscle tissue clung to the inside of the hide and with them fat and hair, yet Donald did not clean the skin.

He went back into the bedroom and took from the woman's bundle the roll of blankets. He returned to the byre and wrapped the blankets around the hide. He found his long cloth coat, and with the hide under his arm, he opened the cottage door and went out into the night.

Fourth Stone

The storm abated and the light of an autumn moon, high over the Atlantic, lit the path as Donald made his way out onto the moor. The tracks were not visible to him but in the distance he could see a faint light from a cottage window, far out on those moors. He knew that the light that shone there came from Mary's cottage and he made for it, stumbling as he went, across the remains of fallen peat banks, and jumping, as best he could, the sodden bog.

Donald had not spoken to his cousin, Mary, since the death of her love rival and her baby. Margaret had wanted him to go and see her, and he knew that his wife thought him weak for his lack of willingness to stand apart from the ignorance of the village mob that had rejected Mary. But Margaret, too, had now grown suspicious of his cousin. The fact was, his son Angus did visit her, and that was enough, for Donald, to keep their kinship alive.

He reached the cottage and finding the door unbolted, he entered without knocking. Mary was sitting on a bench close to the open fire in the centre of the room, her form almost hidden in the mass of brown, acidic smoke that billowed from the burning peat. Apart from the low murmur of the fire the only sound in the cottage was that of a small drum that Mary held and tapped in a slow, steadily insistent beat with a beater made of animal bone. As she played she sang almost in a whisper the words of a song. But words they were not, more to Donald's ears just short noises, odd noises akin to the squeals of small animals, mice, rats and the other creatures that dogged the harvest. She continued playing as Donald came toward her. When he saw her he knew that she too was on the point of starvation. Her face was drawn, her bones protruded almost through the dark leathered flesh of her cheeks.

'Mary,' he said quietly, 'I've come to ask you . . .'

She interrupted, 'I was expecting you, Donald.'

'Mary, I need help, I need to know . . .' he began frantically before she stopped him.

'I know. You want to know if the boy will live, if I can save him . . .'

'Yes,' Donald said, moving across to her with the bundle of cloth and skin, 'I've brought you the hide.'

He placed the hide on the bench beside her and then withdrew, back into the dark smoke that hung about the corners of the room. Mary remained silent and did not lift her eyes from the bright glow of the fire as Donald left the cottage, and made for home.

Mary fasted for two days, and then, as dawn broke on the third day, she took the fresh hide from the bundle and walked towards the shore.

The Atlantic gales brought thunderous waves onto the boulders at the top of the beach. The roar of the waves and the wind, and the screeching gulls that flew above the breaking white water, greeted her.

She unrolled the hide and unbelted the greatcoat she had worn to cross the moor to this, the remotest of the beaches in the district. Beneath the coat she was naked, and naked she stood in the bitter wind. She wrapped the hide around her back and then her arms, and then she lay on the shore above the breaking waves and, finally, covered her face in the skin from the calf's head.

The boy lay in his bed drifting in and out of consciousness. He was silent but for an agitated murmuring and the coughing that grated from his throat.

Donald, knowing that Mary would fast before making for that bay, now stood at the cliff top and looked down at the shore where she lay, wrapped in the hide.

Mary lay enveloped in the hide, with the roar of the ocean and the roar of the wind filling her head. She lay motionless for another day and another night, and, as morning broke, Donald went again to that small bay and stood on the cliff top, looking down at the solitary figure at the shore.

A gathering of gulls stood close to the figure lying by that shore, their beaks facing the gale, their heads tucked close to their braced bodies.

An oystercatcher flew from the rocks and piped as it flew close to the waves, carrying its white cross towards him. 'The *gille brighde*,' thought Donald, 'maybe the child will be saved.'

Mary finally came from the hide, and Donald ran to her, almost falling from the cliffs as he descended the steep, rocky path in hurried expectation. When he reached her, he stood silently before her, his head bowed.

'He will live, Donald. I know he will live,' she said, and Donald, without saying a word, turned and left her on the shore.

Fifth Stone

Donald sat by the fireside. For the first time in many days the cottage was quiet. The sound of the baby crying had stopped and the low, moaning chorus of the storm's raging wind had died back. Margaret stood in the doorway at the far end of the cottage that led to the bedroom.

'Angus is sleeping,' she said, and Donald nodded.

'The storm's going down at last, and what day is it? What bloody day is it?' he asked with bitterness in his voice. 'The Sabbath,' he said, replying to his own question.

He went from the fireside and looked out through the cottage's single window. He could see that the dark mass of grey cloud that had hung above the bay had moved south, leaving in its wake a calming sea and a glint of golden sunlight that flecked and danced on the dark blue ocean.

'The weather's broken at last, but for how long? For how bloody long?'

Margaret stood in silence watching as his temper grew.

'Well, I'll not wait. Sabbath or no Sabbath, I'm not going to let them starve.'

He turned from the window and went to the byre where he kept the long-lines and the heavy, oiled coat he wore fishing in the cold months.

There was then a heavy thumping on the cottage's solid wooden door, and Donald, holding the grey feathers of the line he had started to untangle, came back into the main room and motioned to his wife to open the door.

She lifted the latch and opened the door, suspicious of who might be calling at their house on the Sabbath.

'Margaret, we want to speak to Donald,' said a man whose deep voice Donald recognised. Margaret, without replying to their visitor, opened the door and let him into the room.

The minister stood before Donald, and behind the minister stood two of the village elders, men who not one week before had stood with Donald on the beach as the storm raged, and they had peered out into the wild breaking waves of the bay as though watching, in itself, would help abate the storm. Donald let the long-line fall to his feet.

'You were seen,' began the minister, 'going to that house, and she was seen at the shore.'

'What house would that be now?' replied Donald.

'You know full well which house I mean, Donald, may God forgive you. You've been to Mary's house.'

'And what of it?'

'That woman is cursed by the Devil, and if you don't want to share in her fate, then stay away from her and her work.'

'Is this your doing, Murdan?' asked Donald of one of the elders standing behind the minister. Murdan looked away from Donald's piercing stare, and remained silent, shaking his head.

'Were you not at that house last winter yourself, Alec?' Donald asked of the other man in the party, 'when your wife was in labour?'

'I was, but now I know of the Lord's work . . .'

'Is this storm the Lord's work, too? Is a starving son the Lord's work? Is a boy coughing blood your God's work?' Donald shouted at him.

The minister interjected.

'Enough, Donald, we will not tolerate the men of this village using that woman and her cursed work. Do you understand, Donald? It is up to you if you want to bring shame on this house, or not. But every man in this village relies on this community and if you want to remain a part of it, you will stay away from Mary.'

'Yes, I understand, Minister. I understand very well . . .'

The minister looked at him and then, slowly, turned and ushered the elders out of the cottage. Margaret closed the door behind them, and, weeping, went to the back room.

Donald picked the long-line from the floor, his fist white with tension and anger as he clasped it, and blood ran from his fingers as a hook closed its barb in his fist, piercing his flesh.

He opened his fist and looked at the protruding lump in his palm where the hook's point and barb lay buried beneath his skin. He grabbed the hook's shank and pulled it straight from his skin, ripping

25

the barb through and out. His blood ran brightly, dripping onto the earth floor, but Donald finished cleaning the line, feeling the burn of salt from the cord entering the wound.

'I'm going out,' he called to Margaret, 'Sabbath or no Sabbath!' He took up the sack in which he had packed the line, and headed for the door. Margaret called to him, trying to stop him, but he had left the cottage by the time she could reach the doorway.

Donald walked to the neighbour's cottage and banged on the door.

'John,' he called, finishing his sentence before the door was opened. 'I'm taking the boat out.'

Donald turned and walked toward the shore not waiting for the reply.

The door opened abruptly.

'Donald, wait!'

'I'll not wait John, if we are to catch anything today we must head out now.'

'You can't . . .' said his neighbour.

'And why is that?' said Donald who turned abruptly to face the man. 'Is there not a boat sitting on that shore there waiting to be taken out?'

'It's Sunday, Donald, please think of Margaret.'

'Well, think of it as a necessity, as an act of mercy, John. Aren't your children hungry on a Sunday the same as any other day? This weather is too good to lose. If you're not coming, I'm going alone.'

Donald did not wait to hear the reply. He walked onto the shore aware that the sound of his boots on the stones would drown out any reply his neighbour gave to him.

He took hold of the boat's stern and began to push it towards the ocean, forcing the prow out into the shallow waves that broke on the dark red stones with a thunderous, hushing clatter.

The boat rode before him on the waves, its painted name, *An Sgarbh*, before his face, and Donald pushed out until he was waist-deep in the water. Then, the force of a wave turned the prow back towards the shore and Donald fell beneath the waves. He took hold of the boat again, pushing it forward into the rising and falling of the sea, and then he heard the minister's voice calling to him.

'Donald! You must not take that boat out on the Sabbath.'

But Donald ignored the minister's warnings and pushed on until he heard, above the sound of the breaking waves, running feet on the shore, and somebody making their way out into the waves behind him.

As the noise of raised voices came at him from the shore, he readied himself to tussle with whichever one of their number was going to try to stop him from taking the boat out that day.

Donald pushed on out into the ocean, not bothering to turn and see who it was that was approaching and just as he thought his attacker had reached him he felt the rise of the boat as another pair of hands suddenly joined his own in pushing the boat forward.

'Get in, Donald!' yelled his neighbour, John, above the sound of the sea.

Donald looked at John, 'Aye,' he said, 'let's get her out.'

When both men were in the boat they hoisted the sail on the halyard and the red ochre sheet filled with the remnants of the storm that had kept them on land, and which now pulled them to the open sea. As they went out into the ocean, a flock of gulls gathered behind them, each one, thought Donald, the soul of a starving child.

They guided the boat towards the rocky reef that made entering that bay so hazardous to anyone not familiar with those waters, and Donald let out the first line and they watched it sink beneath into the darkness of the ocean. Then another and another they let out, doing the work of eight men.

Within moments the first long-line was pulling and dragging on the boat's side, and the two men began to pull it in and onto the floor of the boat. The first hooks flashed and quivered with the silver and dark-blue tiger patterns of the mackerel.

The fish bled their thick, dark red blood onto the hands of the fishermen and onto the boat's open timbers. Beneath the boat, a frenzy of feeding and death had erupted. Fish came on board; some were gaffed through the eye and others, the fin. Sometimes, more than one came on each hook with one pierced in the mouth and the other in the tail.

The two men pulled on the lines, freeing the fish from the large hooks, and the fish fell into the boat, flapped and curled until death froze them in a rigid, locked bend, head to tail.

The fishermen pulled and grasped at the line, their hands catching on the open hooks that gashed their flesh. John looked at his blood-covered neighbour and saw that there were tears running down his face as they emptied that line.

'Thank God, John. Thank God,' said Donald.

When the seas had fallen quiet and the lines had been emptied and returned to the boat, they turned towards the shore. Neither man had looked back at the village as they fished, and both now looked at the crowd that had gathered and had witnessed their fight with the line and the ocean, and the effort of bringing in a large catch.

'It'll be all right, John,' Donald tried to reassure his younger neighbour.

As they approached the beach and jumped into the shallow water to guide the boat and its catch to safety, they heard the ranting of the minister, warning the gathered crowd to disperse and return home. But they did not go, and stood in silence, ignoring the angry commands being yelled at them by their minister.

'If God had not meant them to fish today, why is the boat full?' asked one of the waiting villagers in a low voice to his neighbour.

When the two fishermen reached the shore and the boat was grounded on the glistening stones, all stood in silence. The minister looked at the men and their heavy catch of mackerel; the men and women of the village stood in silence, fearful of the minister, but each knew that the catch would be shared out amongst them all.

An elderly woman finally moved forward and Donald took a fish from the boat and dropped it into her empty basket; then the crowd moved forward, and the menfolk of the village helped Donald and his neighbour empty the boat and haul it to the dry slopes of the beach. The catch was shared among them all.

As baskets were filled the minister turned and walked away from the crowd, and that night, for the first time in a month, the households of the village slept quietly, undisturbed by the crying of children in pain.

Sixth Stone

Mary came to the cottage knowing that the man and wife of that house would be out in the fields. Under her arm she carried the rolled hide. She entered the small dwelling and found Angus playing on the hard dirt floor in the dim interior.

'Come on', she whispered, hurrying the boy to his feet and knowing that he trusted her and would go with her without the risk of a commotion that would attract attention to her plans.

'Where are we going?' he asked her.

'To the falls,' she replied, 'but we must not be seen.'

Angus came out of the cottage with her and they walked the banks of the river that crossed the fields in a steep glen. The banks were clotted with stunted trees, birch, rowan, a struggling, twisted hazel and stands of willow that spiked fresh green fronds from a gnarled stump.

In that glen their passage could not be seen from the fields and the two walked in silence until Mary stopped at Linn Dubh, on the banks of a great pool beneath a waterfall. Rainwater still flooded the rivers and the falls roared with deafening force.

Mary unrolled the hide on the banks of the pool and laid Angus down upon it, and she too then lay on the hide and wrapped it about them both, pulling in the ends until all daylight was banished from beneath its covers and all that filled their senses was the roar of the falls.

Inside the hide she took from her pocket a small rolled cloth and from it she brought four carved teeth, two for the child and two for her own mouth. She opened the child's mouth and placed the whale teeth behind the gums, such that the tips would protrude from his lips.

Donald returned home from the fields. He entered the cottage.

'Angus!' he called, 'Angus, come here and help me with this load!'

But no reply came. Donald stood back into the daylight and walked around the back of the cottage, but did not find the boy.

'Margaret,' he called down the lane to his wife, 'did Angus go with us to the fields?'

'No', came the reply and for a moment they stood silently looking at each other, and then as realisation took hold in them both, Margaret fell to her knees and half-sobbing yelled at her husband, 'Stop her, stop her!'

Donald, now ashen with fear and anger, ran into the village, calling the names of the men in each of the houses to help him. A party quickly assembled on the street.

'Mary has taken the child,' Donald said to the crowd. 'She's taken him.'

'Are you sure?' asked one.

'Aye, I'm sure,' he said more quietly, resigned to the humiliation he foresaw in her actions.

'Where? Where would she take the boy?' They asked him, not needing to ask 'why'.

'The shore, the linn, perhaps, anywhere there's water.'

'God help him now,' said another, 'we must find them.'

As they prepared to begin their search, Margaret came to her husband.

'I told you not to go near that woman, 'she spat. 'She's taken our child, she's got him and it's your fault.'

Donald made no reply, turned and joined the other men as they set out for the moor.

'To the shore,' Donald called to them, 'head for the shore, the bay below Beinn Ruadh!'

It was the bay that Mary had chosen when Donald had gone to her with the hide.

They reached the steep cliffs above that bay but found its sands to be empty.

While the men searched the moor, Margaret returned to the cottage. As she stood in the darkness, the thought came to her, a vision, perhaps, of Mary and the boy by the falls.

She went to the byre and picked up the large bone-handled knife that Donald had used to skin the calf for the hide and began to walk the glen toward Linn Dubh.

As she drew nearer, she saw the hide by the falls. In its form she could see the outline shapes of the bodies it contained and her fingers turned the handle of the knife slowly in her fist.

Margaret walked over to the form lying by the falls. She saw no movement, and no sound came from within the hide. She raised the knife high above her head but waited before plunging it downwards. She lowered the knife and drew back the fold of skin that covered the face of the boy. She saw the teeth protruding from his mouth and fainting backwards screamed and lunged with the knife at the other body.

The knife held firm in the cut it had made in the hide and blood slowly seeped around its handle. Neither woman nor child moved. Margaret turned and ran back up the glen. As she ran a crow flew by her, cawing in anger.

As she reached the top of the glen Margaret saw the party of men approaching. She led them to the pool and the hide lying there.

When the men arrived at that scene they found no trace of the woman, and only the boy lay wrapped in the hide, the whale teeth still in his mouth and two others in his hands.

Donald took the teeth from the boy's mouth and hands and hurled them to the river.

Seventh Stone

A single, bright star hung in the eastern sky as the first beacons of torch flame appeared over the north moorland horizon. Beneath the faint orange glow moved the black form of a loosely ordered mob, approaching the township.

From east and west across the moor, single specks of flamelight moved toward the approaching mob and one by one their light was subsumed into the growing mass of light as the mob grew.

Donald stood in the doorway of the cottage and looked about the silent village. The church door was open and the white-yellow light of candles faintly illuminated the building from within.

On the easternmost flank of the village was the Bard's Well and there, huddled and busy, was another gathering of men moving the stone slab that covered the well's small, clear pool. By the well, a curl of light grey smoke drifted into the sky in a twisting column from a fierce spot of firelight at its base.

The mob neared and as they neared so lights showed in the small windows of more and more of the village's cottages. Out on the moor, curlews piped their solitary note into the morning air, as startled grouse blustered a low flight to safety.

Then, they too were silenced by the sound of feet upon the track. Closer still the procession came to the village and human voices could then be heard. Loudest among them was the sound of a man shouting wildly. As the procession drew closer still, the sound of a woman's voice could also be heard and she too was shouting.

Donald bowed his head as he thought, with trepidation, of the events to come. For the first time in his own memory, one of his own people had been taken from her cottage on the moor and it was her voice he now heard; it was her screaming. It was, he thought, a cruel fate of coincidence that the first spring procession his first son would see would be that at which one of his own kin was being hauled before the parish. But Donald's heart was cold towards the yelling woman.

His wife joined Donald in the doorway of the cottage.

'Go back inside . . .' Donald said, without looking at her, 'and send Angus to me, clothed as he should be. The boy's old enough now.'

'No, Donald, Angus is still a child', pleaded Margaret.

'Get him. He has to learn.'

'The fright will kill him, he is only a child,' she protested.

'I told you yesterday. He will see it this year. He will see it before it is all gone for good and I will not allow my son to be the only boy in this village who . . .' Donald broke off his talk when he noticed that his wife had gone from the doorway.

They had argued about the procession almost since the birth of their first son and, on this subject, Donald was at his most obstinate and his wife had once said that she barely recognised him when they talked of the procession.

He turned his head into the still unlit interior of the house.

'The children of this village almost starved this last winter. Is that what you want?'

But no reply came from within the house.

Moments later, dressed in black, as was his father that morning, the figure of a small boy emerged into the light and stood in the doorway, his mother holding his hand.

'Go inside, I said, and stay there. Angus will stay here with me now; he'll stay here with me alone,' Donald commanded and Margaret, letting go of the boy's hand, went into the dark room.

'Stay with me and we'll watch them passing,' said Donald to his son.

'Who is that coming so early?' asked the small boy, pointing at the procession.

'They're coming to the well and to the church,' said Donald and then man and boy stood in silence as the procession closed on the boundary of the township.

'Look,' said the boy suddenly, 'why is Mary with them? Why are they pulling her like that?'

'Because she has to be.'

'Why don't you tell him the truth?' said Margaret from inside the house. 'Why, if he must witness this cruelty, don't you tell him the truth about it.'

'He would not understand,' replied Donald.

'No, that's not it. You don't understand and you're too much of a coward to stop them from taking your own cousin, that's the truth. You could stop this if you wanted to, you know that, but you're too weak to stand up to them. At the end of last year it could have been you they were hauling down that road.'

'Be quiet!' Donald yelled into the house, closing the door behind his words.

The small boy and his father then stood in silence as the procession approached them. At the front were a handful of men and a roped woman who stumbled as she was pulled down the track, her eyes wide with horror. Her mouth was open, hanging open with the tiredness of constant shouting.

Behind them, in solemn silence, walked men from the southern, eastern and western townships and as the procession passed the houses of the north people, so the men of the north joined its ranks and the column made its way up to the church, the well and the growing fire.

As the procession neared their door, the small boy clung to his father's legs and tried to hide there, shutting out all sight of the procession, his free hand tight against his ear. But Donald turned the boy firmly to the front and held his hands from his face, opening his ears to the noise.

'Mary!' cried the boy, tugging on his father's hand in an effort to reach the woman as she approached them at the front of the line.

'Be silent!' yelled Donald, pulling the child back as the procession reached them.

The small boy was ashen in the face by the time the crowd passed their door. Mary looked at Donald and the boy, tears were now running down her face, and she turned away. His father then pulled the boy onto the road and they joined the column of people. The small boy walked with his father dragging his feet with reluctant steps, in silence and sick with fear.

The procession neared the Bard's Well and the fire crackled loudly as dried sea timbers smoked and caught, glowing with bright orange flame. The procession then stopped and Angus watched as the men at the well came forward and doused each of the captives with the well water. As the water ran down their faces, an elderly man spoke loudly to the crowd of evil and forgiveness and of the banishment of madness, but at the well, the name of God was not heard.

The captives were then led through the gathered crowd who turned and followed, back towards the church. Those at the front no longer struggled as they walked to the dark stone form of the ancient church building. At its side, a rough wooden door was already open and they were led into a small, low-roofed ante-chapel, and the door was locked behind them.

The procession then formed again and went back towards the well and the flame. A cauldron was placed upon the fire and a dozen cups each of barley, purple heather tops and white withered carrot flowers were flung into the water when it had finally boiled.

'That is all for now, Angus.'

'We will return when the brew is finished and you will walk with me again. We'll walk into the waves and spill the ale there, in the hope of getting a good year. Think of all the barrels full of salt fish set by for when the days shorten again.'

Angus was silent as they walked back home. Margaret came to the door as they approached. Angus broke free of his father's hand and ran to the embrace of his mother, who looked at Donald in disgust.

Eighth Stone

The village air was full of the smell of burnt barley all that day, and for the remainder of that week the acrid smell of fermentation was a constant reminder of the tension and anticipation many felt about the events that were to come. The ale fermented silently in the now capped cauldron. A small light of fire was kept beneath it to speed the transformation of the brew, and each morning, village men would stir the liquid with scrubbed oars as it smoked into the cold air of dawn.

When the day came, Donald, Margaret and Angus went to the church together and joined the other villagers in prayers for the mad. The captives remained locked in the side chapel, barely visible to the congregation, as they peered through the narrow stone slit windows that connected the small side chapel with the main body of the church.

Then, one by one, each of the tormented souls was led out before the parish, forced to their knees and made to seek forgiveness before being given a blessing. And each did in turn and each was forgiven, led away, and freed into the bright daylight until only one remained. One who, in her weakness, could not speak and who fell to her face when forced to her knees, and who lay motionless and mute before the congregation.

Angus heard the silence of the church broken by the minister's repeated demands of her to plead for her own forgiveness. But she could not. Angus watched as she was finally carried from that place back to the small chapel.

'What will they do with her?' asked the boy.

'They'll set her free later', came the reply, 'when darkness comes, they will set her free.'

The service finished and the procession gathered again outside the church. Donald held his son's hand firmly in his own as the women of the village were sent away home. The procession of men then went to the cauldron. Its heavy stone cap was lifted, and the pungent smell of the fermented ale filled the air.

Each man took his cup and filled it with ale, and then, when each had their offering in their cup, the procession started towards the shore and the quiet rolling waves of the Atlantic.

As they reached the first shallow waves the sky was full of a tumult of seagulls, raised from their cliff ledges by the sound of the approaching procession. The white flashes of a thousand beating wings, blinding and brilliant filled the bright blue sky.

The village men took up their cups and walked into the ocean, calling for a bounteous harvest; calling for the gift of abundance from the north waters, and as they pleaded, so they spilt the ale into the waves. All then returned home. There was talk of the spring work starting within a week.

As darkness settled and the boy and his father sat by a warming fire, the calm that was returning to the household was disturbed by a sudden and unexpected knocking. Barely audible at first, and then more frantic, the knocking grew harder and more insistent until Donald went to the door.

'Who is it?' he demanded from inside. But no reply came and he opened the door. The darkness of the night was in the sky but nobody could be seen in his doorway.

'Who's there?' asked the boy's father once again. 'Is that you, Mary?' he called fiercely and forbiddingly into the darkness. But no reply came. 'What do you want here?' he asked, but still no reply came.

Donald returned inside the cottage and closed and locked the door behind him.

'There's nothing we can do for her,' he said before anyone else could speak.

Angus went from his fireside stool, and peered out into the darkness from the small glazed window beside the door. He thought he saw the form of a woman walking beside the road outside the cottage, a woman holding the top stones of the field wall to steady herself as she went on her way.

For a fleeting moment, she turned her face towards the cottage and Angus, seeing that it was Mary, called to his mother, 'It is her, it is her, it's Mary, she's outside! Let her in!'

'No,' bellowed his father, 'we will not! Come away from that window before I put the belt to you.'

Angus turned again and looked out to where he had seen her standing, staring at their cottage, but she was gone.

But Angus could not forget her; he could not forget the days he had spent with her out on the moor. He could not forget the days they spent together that were full of stories. He could not forget how she spoke, and he heard her speak again as his thoughts went back to those days. He could feel the cool breeze of July ghosting into the dark interior of that remote cottage.

The breeze was pungent with meadow flowers and fuelled by the sound of the nearby river. Daylight flowed through the low wooden door that was pegged to the wall of the cottage front for most of the summer months. At times, Mary's words railed, fierce as winter hail. She spoke with wildness in her eyes, a wild anger even, but at other times she spoke with love and tenderness, and then he felt close to her.

But now she was gone and forgotten by all but one, the small boy who, tormented in his sleep, saw that she was dead. The night she had been to their cottage but had not got in, he saw her in his dreams. He saw her floating on the open sea and then going beneath the waves, her body face down, her hair drifting on the surface.

He woke the following morning, and for the first time in his life he was aware of feeling hatred. He had hatred for his father. Now, the venom and tantrums for which he was renowned as a small boy were turned against his father. He hated him with beating fists and with a barely suppressed yelling. If he could have thought of the words, if he could remember those words he was not allowed to say, he would have hurled them at his father.

In the quietness of the byre, where the small boy had made a corner for himself with old rags and sea timbers, he wept for Mary.

A week after the procession and the night-time visitation at their cottage, Angus had gone to a remote corner of the shore, beyond the jutting, weed-covered rocks that fell from the low hills out into the waves, and was sitting on the shore watching the slow loping of seals on and off the flat, grey mounds out in the waves. As he watched, he could see that the seals and gulls were agitated by the advance of an object in the water that slowly came in on the waves until, in the shallows, he could see that it was the bloated and bruised body of a woman.

He walked towards the floating object, his heart pounding in his chest, not thinking about who it could be, and, as it slowly came in and stopped where the waves ended their slow breaking movement over the beach, he saw that it was Mary.

He stood looking down at the body. Frozen with fear, his hands shook, and slowly the tremor moved from his hands and through his arms until it was in his face. His jaw quivered and a tear broke from the corner of his eye, and it was followed by yet more until there was a stream of burning salt, molten, emanating from the core of his emotion. The hard tears ran down his face and he fell to his knees. He wanted to embrace her, to kiss her cheek as he had that of his grandfather when he had seen him laid out in a rough wooden coffin, in a pure white *marbh-phaisg*.

As he reached forward he was also revolted by the sight of her battered and bloated body. He felt disgust with himself but still he wanted to hold her. But he could not bring himself to do so. He could not even take her hand, and he turned away. He could not run, either. He could not leave her there, alone on the sands, open to the violence of the now beguiling waves.

He turned back and knelt again at her side, and his hands clawed at the sodden sand. He heard her voice. She was again in the house. He was sitting on a long dark bench that ran nearly the full length of one wall of the small main room of the reed-roofed cottage. His eyes were heavy, and he was half-intoxicated by the acridness of the peat smoke that came from the open fire in the middle of the floor. The smoke gathered in corners, and hung in a layer, dividing in two the scant light in the room. Above him was a dark impenetrable layer in which the heads of adults appeared as though from nothingness. Below him, a clearer, less choking space. If he lay on the bench he was almost entirely in that clear space and could watch the heat of the fire glowing through the pyramid of large peats that burned continually.

He heard Mary talking in a low, droning voice as though she were imparting secret knowledge in words that must not be overheard by anyone in the next room. But there was no one there to overhear her *procaid*. The words reflected the weight of her tale, and everything she told him seemed to be both true and false at the same time, as though she spoke only in and through myths.

Or, perhaps, it was that everything in her life was mythology. She had, like almost all others of her generation, led a self-mythologising life in which the imagination fabricated reality as a dark and threatening place, echoing with the billowed grandeur of biblical Gaelic. You were not born, you were begotten. The archaic and primal were places reserved for this grand language, and so too was her own history, and that of the generations she spoke of, who had gone before her.

As the sound of the waves slowly broke back into his consciousness, he realised that he was kneeling in the shallow break of a long wave. The story he heard that day in the smoke broke too; broke over his imagination. Mary was cursing loudly; cursing the one who had put the *mallachadh* on her, and from which she had never been able to free herself.

As a young girl, she explained, she had been drawn to the son of the tacksman, and years later, in the privacy of her own cottage, she cursed the day she had ever set eyes on him.

Ailean Ruadh had none of the ruthless, cruel streak his father showed toward the poor cotters, who, like her, struggled to survive on a bare stony patch, stolen from the rough grazing at the moor side. He would often, hearing of the threats his father made to those people, call on them, and reassure them.

Mary's home was one at which he was a frequent visitor, and she felt encouraged that he was showing more interest in her than in the affairs of his father's business. He would call and sit on the bench by the fire. He would ask kindly after the family, and he would talk proudly, and in a louder voice than most of the tenants, about agriculture and the new methods.

Once a year he would come to the house with good meat from the animals he had stalked across the north moorland. He would enter the cottage still bloodied from the kill and deliver to them the leg or haunch of the beast.

But Mary had a rival for his affections, and one day, unexpectedly the rival called at the house. In a friendly but over-familiar tone she spoke to Mary about Ailean Ruadh. She spoke coarsely about him, and about love, and how she dreamt of going with him out onto the moors or to the rolling machair, far from the village. As she spoke, and saw that her words brought a blush to Mary's face, she brought from her pocket a lace handkerchief and gave it to Mary as a gift.

Mary took it, but as she took it in her hand she felt a sudden shrieking pain in her fingers. They had been pierced by something hidden in the delicate, sharp-edged folds of the cloth. Her fingers bled onto the lace, and as she opened out the cloth she saw in its folds a needle that had been concealed. Her rival gave her a half-laughing apology for forgetting that that was where she had kept her sharpest needle.

But Mary knew that she had been cursed and her rival had beaten her. In the following weeks, the flesh around the wound festered and rotted until, when it finally healed, she was left without feeling in one finger. Her grasped fist had been weakened, and with it her hold on the intentions of her would-be lover. As she spoke to Angus at the fireside, she held out her finger, and there was a white gash in her otherwise dark skin. She pressed the wound and it did not flush with the blood, it stayed white, and she closed her fist and the finger protruded slightly from the curve in her joints.

Within a year, Mary's rival was carrying a child and Ailean Ruadh had left the district. But, neither mother nor child survived the birth, and far from being the one whom most in the village felt sorrow for, Mary was blamed for cursing her rival.

Mary was returning home from the moor carrying peats in a basket, tied high on her back.

As she walked, her fingers worked at knitting. Suddenly, from the byre of the first house on that side of the moor, a dog came running towards her. Mary knew that dog well and she walked on expecting the usual boisterous welcome. But, on that day, it came at her as though she were an intruder in that part; it came at her baring its teeth and snarling before it jumped at her, its teeth gashing her face. Mary had not been able to free her hands from their work in time, and neither had the dog's master realised the actions of the beast. Finally, hearing a commotion, he came from the house and called the dog away. But Mary noticed that he did not beat or thrash the dog, as was normal when an animal attacked, but took it inside the byre and closed the door, not bothering to tend to the wounds of the victim, and Mary knew that she would be blamed, too, for unsettling the dog.

She was cursed and therefore carried evil with her in the form a dog could sense. Her curse clung to her, and with the fate of her rival no local man would go near her. When Mary married, she did so away from the village, and her marriage was cursed.

Ninth Stone

Angus's eyes focused far out in the waves where white birds flew on the wing and then, with a brilliant flash, dived to the water, their wings folded, their necks extended, and he felt again the cool sea water against his legs.

He looked down at Mary's body. She had drifted away from him a little and was rising and falling as the shallow waves broke under her remains.

He had found her where the ocean leaves lyart timbers, high on the shore. He had found her where stone and sand collide and where in the dark winter falling rocks clatter from the high cliffs into the sea.

He had found her body where the bird tide leaves its kerf and where storm-wrenched seaweed lies scattered in tresses. She lay there, her eyes open but unseeing. Her mouth too was open but she was silent now. Her hair lay about her like torn kelp, in long strands draped, blood red on the shore.

She lay among the shallow pools the ebb forgot. Beneath a sigh of cloud she lay, beak-carved, indifferent in death to the roup of skuas, her hands reddened with rock blood.

The small boy took a fistful of the sand from where she lay and held it until it was again a boulder of wind-cut granite falling to the sea from the northern cliffs.

And then another fist of sand he held until it was a stone journeying in a river far inland, flowing among frost-split boulders.

The small boy held that river in his hands until it was again a mountain glacier burdened with a moraine as it clove the island glens.

Beneath a sigh of cloud, her hands reddened with rock blood, the body of the woman lay on the shore among shallow pools the ebb forgot.

Tenth Stone

For as long as the secret of Mary's return remained with him, Angus returned to that remote corner of the shore. Some days her body was not there and the beach seemed depleted. On these days he would remain, feeling the cold wind in his face and watching the milling and probing of larks among the clumps of seaweed that lagged, deserted by the tide, and he saw the dazzle of oystercatchers roving the breaking waves. Maybe she would be gone for a day or more and then she would return to some place beyond his reach or close to where she might be seen from the village. And when she was there he would sit by her, and each time that she returned to the beach, she had been more wounded by the sea. Her face was all but lost, but still Angus would sit with her, wishing to hold her hand as though that would give her comfort. But he could not. Her eyes were gashed and exposed to their sockets, open and forbidding, locked in a cold trauma.

As he sat on the beach with her remains he could still hear her voice as she told him stories of the local men and women, and of the sorrows that had bereaved her. She had had a husband once, and had a son, both of whom were lost to the sea in a storm that came suddenly to a summer day. Their boat had gone out from the harbour in fine weather, and no one could have guessed the severity of the weather that closed on the northern seas that day.

The sole survivor of that wrecking told her the fate of husband and son. As soon as the bad weather had come in, he told her, they had made for a small grass-and-sand island not ten miles from the north west of the island. They made it to dry land but within an hour a giant wave had washed over that small island, taking with it all but one of the fishermen.

He, the storyteller, had been carried by the force of the water but had lodged, by chance, in a fold on the dunes. The island had been cut in two by the force of the wave, and it was three days before a passing boat saw his frantic attempts to attract attention and he was saved. The bodies of her husband and son were never found.

Mary would talk of her son to Angus, and as she did so she would place her arm about his shoulders, and tell him that her son would now have been thirty, if he had not gone to sea that day.

Angus's mother and father knew that he had found Mary but they did not know that he was returning to the beach every day to be with her body.

They thought that he had at last made friends within the village and was away playing in the rock pools or fishing from the rocks with the other boys. But he always returned alone; he never brought home fish and never spoke of the adventures they thought he was having.

The truth was that he was a withdrawn and self-conscious boy. Most thought it was a miracle that he ever spoke a word, such was the distance he put between himself and others of his age. He cried more tears than he spoke words, and most were not surprised when it came out that he had made a friend of the dead woman.

One night, Angus had again returned to the beach. He had taken with him that night the river net his father used for catching salmon.

He had taken it to Mary's body and had thrown it over her where she lay. He had waited for her body to come up on the right part of the shore, nearer to the caves at the beach end, and, that night, she had drifted in on the tide.

With a monumental effort he had dragged her in the net the short distance across the sands into the darkness of the cave mouth. There he had covered her in dry cave stones, and marked the burial place with driftwood.

But his father had seen him take the net from the house, and with two or three others – including an uncle maybe not more than ten years Angus's senior – he had gone to the cave, and found Angus covering the body.

Angus fought and struggled with them, screaming and kicking as they tried to pull him away from her. Held in the arms of his uncle, he saw them take her from the cave and return her to the waves, and that was the last he ever saw of her.

His father took him home and beat him for having brought shame upon the house, and Angus went to his bed wishing evil on him.

In darkness, at the door of his small bedroom, he listened to his parents' raised voices. His mother and father were arguing, and his mother was blaming his father for the trouble that had come to their door since the day of the procession. Maybe, she reasoned, it was the shock Angus had taken that day, watching Mary being taken by the mob.

As he slept that night, Angus saw in his dreams his father's face grimacing with fear and anguish as he fought to stay above the waves. His arm was reaching towards a boat, but he remained beyond the reach of the grasping hands on board.

Then his father was gone beneath the waves. And that is how the small boy learnt to use the gift of sight.

Successive generations of the family had lost their menfolk at sea. That much Angus knew, and within a few months of that traumatic night and its visitation of dreams, Angus's father had died, drowned whilst fishing, as foreseen by the boy.

His body was washed up on the shore some months later – and there it remained. It, like Mary's, was disfigured and bloated, and the flesh had been tugged at by dolphins or seals and hung loosely from soft-edged wounds.

But the boy did not sit with the body of his father. He did not take the net from the rafters and try to drag him away, or bury him in a cave. His body was left at the water's edge, in the hinterland of shore and sea, where the sands were deepest.

The body lay there, watched by a patrol of skuas that would prod and probe at the flesh, but would not wholeheartedly eat of the corpse. Perhaps, he thought, even they found it impossible to approach. Then, after a high tide, the body was gone and did not return.

Eleventh Stone

On the night that his father's body had been found on the beach, Angus saw in his sleep the face of the young uncle who took him, with his father, away from Mary's body in the cave. He too was struggling for breath, his head above and then beneath the waves, above and then again beneath the waves. As he came to the air his yelling was frantic but there was no outstretched hand to help him. He was alone in the waves.

He was alone beside an empty boat. And then he was gone beneath the waves and his head did not rise again, and the yelling ceased, leaving a fractured silence hanging above the sea, breaking the calmness of the day.

One month later the body of the uncle returned to the beach. There was no boy there waiting to look over him. Neither father nor uncle ever had the vigil of love the boy had kept over Mary.

Mary had told Angus that when a fisherman went missing overboard, or did not return from a solo voyage, he could have gone voluntarily to the depths. He may have gone with the seagulls or the seals when times were hard on dry land, lured by the promise of a land of plenty beneath the waves: a land where he could live an idyllic life of abundance, having abandoned his family to struggle for survival alone. To save them, he must journey, too, and free their souls from the evil that held them.

They would not be buried when they came back to land for fear that the burial would encourage others down that selfish path. Some thought that the bodies might have been sent from the depths to live on land, to lure others away to that place. But if a man chose that path then the circle of his evil would not be closed by a blessed burial on land.

Twelfth Stone

Except for the consoling presence of Angus and the young baby, Margaret was, after the drowning of the menfolk, alone in the house.

Some in the village said it was grief, or shame or both, but more likely it was the relentless hard work on the land and with the animals that caused her own health to fail. She worked in all weathers; doing the work demanded simply for their survival, and then, one day, she collapsed in the field.

Margaret was taken to her bed and tended by the elder womenfolk of the village, some half-cousins, some closely related, others not very related at all. Angus saw his mother half-conscious, drifting in and out of life. She suffered in the dark, unlit interior of the cottage, breathing the acrid smoke of the peat fires, eating nothing, and drinking only a little water.

But, against the odds, she slowly recovered and a day came when Angus was made ready for a journey. With his mother, Angus mounted the low-sided, horse-drawn cart and they were led across the island to a place on the east, a place of golden shores and rolling moorland where the mainland mountains could be seen across the sea.

When they reached the main village on the east side, a healer came to the cart and took mother and son to the side of an open peat cut. He had already started a fire blazing there, and in it, glowing orange with the heat, was a small casket bubbling with a silvery black liquid.

There in the wet ground the healer made the mould of a heart and filled it with the molten lead. The heart was left in the ground to cool and for the metal to set and for their mumbled prayers to work. But God's name was not heard in those prayers.

Angus and his mother then left for home, travelling north on the cart. A week went by, and then Margaret and her son returned to the healer and Margaret took the heart and wrapped it in cloth. Together, Margaret, Angus and the healer went to the sea cliffs and Margaret threw the heart to the waves. As it sank, Margaret's scarred heart was to heal. But it healed for only a year and by the following winter Angus was alone.

His mother's death came suddenly, late on a day that the north wind had covered with snow and a shifting glaze of small hard hailstones that blew in the wind like desert sand, cutting sharp lines and ridges in the white ground. Margaret was out at the back of the house throwing large peats from a tumbled stack into a bulging basket she had saved for the carrying of fuel when it had become useless for any other work.

Angus sat in by the fire not thinking of time passing, and the amount of time that had already passed, when he became aware that his mother had not returned with the load.

He wrapped himself in the large shawl his mother often used when she went out in the bad weather. On this occasion, in her hurry to get the peats in before real darkness came to the day, she had left it behind. Angus went to the back of the house expecting to see his mother standing there, pulling dry black peats from a hole in the stack.

When he turned the corner, and felt the full force of the winter wind in his face, he saw her there, lying slumped against the stack, her face bleeding where she had fallen, and her legs buckled beneath her in such a way that she was half-kneeling. The basket was on its side and the peats had fallen in the snow.

He ran to her, not thinking that she could be dead. He picked up the basket and put the ice-covered peats back inside. He put his arm around her but as he did so her legs gave way and she fell against him. Her weight, light as she was, was too much for the boy and he fell down with her.

Her eyes, like Mary's when he had found her on the beach, were open but with a blank stare and somehow the colour had already drained from them such that they looked as though they were the wax eyes of the doll his mother had made for their neighbour's girl.

Angus pulled his legs free from under his mother's body, and ran, yelling, toward their neighbour's cottage. An old man came to the door and quickly the old man and his son ran to the spot beside the peats where the woman lay. The younger man picked her from the snow and carried her into the house, laying her out on the bed. But it was plain to all who saw her that she was gone, that her heart would beat no more.

His mother was buried in the cemetery by the sea, and Angus then lived alone with the help of his mother's surviving relatives in the village, and a neighbour took the baby.

Thirteenth Stone

A man, maybe in his late thirties, is in a barn, a stone barn with a thatched roof. He is bending over a calf that lies on the floor of the byre; its mother stands beside it, anxiety in her eyes. The cow is uneasy and shuffles her feet among the scattered hay on the floor.

Watched by a more elderly man who pats and strokes the anxious cow, the younger man runs his hands over the calf's leg. As he straightens the calf's leg he is muttering words, his words are unheard by the elderly man.

A young woman comes to the byre door. 'Angus,' she says, addressing the young man.

'What is it, Christina?' he replied, angry at being disturbed.

'Sorry, I'm sorry, Angus, only there is someone at the house asking for you.'

Angus did not reply. He returned to the calf's leg and his nearly silent mutterings.

The elderly man carried on stroking the cow as the young man worked.

The young woman stood awkwardly in the doorway.

'Angus,' she began again, 'she says she must see you urgently.'

'Can't it wait?' Angus barked angrily at her.

'I don't think it can.'

Angus straightened his back and looked at the elderly man.

'I'm sorry,' he said, 'but I have to go. She should be all right now.'

'Aye, son, thank you,' replied the elderly man. 'It was a bad break,' he added as the calf slowly raised itself onto its legs.

'Yes, the bone was right out. But she should be fine now,' said Angus, turning to leave the byre with his wife.

'Before you go, Angus . . .'

'I told you before, I don't want anything for this,' interjected Angus.

'No, no, I know what you said but I've kept this for you, it's from the bull. I think he would have wanted you to have it,' said the elderly man with a slight, ironic smile at the side of his mouth.

He went into the corner of a stall at the back of the byre and dragged a large, rolled hide out from the darkness.

'I thought it might be of use to you.'

Angus looked at the elderly man, and then moved to help him drag the skin.

'Aye,' said Angus, 'I'll bring the cart down for it later.'

'Very good,' said the elderly man as the calf walked about the byre with no trace of its injuries now showing.

'Very good.'

Angus returned home with Christina. The door to the cottage was open and inside, close to the peat fire in the middle of the floor, sat a young woman, Ceit nighean Domhnall Mac Domhnall 'An Tobar'. Angus knew her as the daughter of one of the men of the village, now long dead, who, when Angus was a boy had joined the procession against Mary.

'Ceit,' acknowledged Angus with a stiffness in his voice.

'Angus,' she replied, with a not distant tone of desperation in her voice.

'What is it, Ceit, that brings you here?'

'I need help, Angus . . . help,' and as the words came from her mouth she began to sob. Christina went forward and comforted her.

'I can still hear the voice of another coming from years back now who wanted help, who wanted saving and I can see still your father's face, Ceit, turned against her.'

'Angus,' interjected his wife in a scalding tone, 'the child is nearly dead, if not lying dead as we speak. This is not the time to settle that issue.'

Angus did not reply.

'Did anyone see you coming here, Ceit?' Asked his wife.

'No, not a soul, I'm sure of that.'

'What do you want me to do?' asked Angus knowing full well what her request would be.

'The child is dying, gasping for breath,' began Ceit but was unable to finish.

'What can I do?'

'Save him, Angus, please try and save him.'

'I cannot. I cannot. That just puts this house at risk, puts us all at risk.'

'I know you can, I've always known that.'

'Angus, you must try and help her,' said his wife.

Angus stood in silence looking at the two women on the floor. His wife held the crying mother. Burnt peat shifted on the fire, its grey-white ash falling to the side and exposing a glowing, orange-red heart.

Angus went to the door and looked out over the fields towards the machair. The low, hunched form of the stone-built church looked black against the clear sky. The village was silent save for the birds calling from the moors. In the calling of the birds he heard his mother's voice, his father's voice and Mary's voice. He saw the stormy night on which his father had crossed the moor to Mary's cottage to save the baby. He heard that baby coughing, its lungs choked with fever. He saw the distant shore and the form lying there in the animal skin. He was again inside the calf skin with Mary, close to the falls. Beyond their cocoon by that pool was silence, but inside Mary was muttering, growling, her eyes remote, lost in some other place and he was with her there, below the sea where souls gathered. In the mountains where souls gathered, in the sky where souls soar, they flew, they dived, they walked in high places among boulders glazed with white ice and at their side ran fox and wolf, swam whale and salmon, flew crow and gull, and Mary spoke with them in barks and cries and other sounds not known to him. But then he knew them, he heard them almost as words.

At a cave they stopped and saw people sitting by a fire. The eldest came forward and Mary pleaded with her for the return of the youngest seated there, and the youngest came back with them to the cottage, the familiar cottage, their home in the village and life was back in the child who coughed again, who cried, and who was back from the dead.

Then they were under the waves, walking not swimming, walking on the sea floor, not bothering with breath or air and Mary left Angus at the mouth of a hole that sank far into the seabed beneath them. He heard her in the blackness, heard her asking for shoals of fish, for seals and whales and shells in abundance to be with them that season and they went back to the shore and saw boats heavy with their catch struggling on towards the harbour.

Angus turned back inside the cottage and saw the two women still huddled on the floor.

'All right,' he said. 'All right, I'll come to the child.'

Ceit, hearing his words, cried more heavily.

51

'Thank you, Angus, thank you.'

Angus hitched the horse to the small cart and started out towards the old man's byre. By the roadside stood the minister who watched as the cart slowly pulled along the track.

'It's the Devil's work Angus,' he said. 'If you want friends in this village you'll turn back.'

Angus looked at him and then turned away and urged the horse on.

The old man greeted him.

'I knew you'd come sooner rather than later,' he said.

'Aye, I've no choice now.'

'That's right, you've no choice.'

The two struggled to lift the hide onto the back of the cart. Angus went back along the road and he saw that the minister was gone, and all was quiet.

'Go home now,' he said to Ceit, 'and make sure that nobody sees you; take the glen road if necessary.'

'Yes, thank you, Angus.'

Ceit went and behind her she left a house preoccupied with fear.

'I've no choice, have I, Christina?'

'No, Angus, you've no choice. It must be done for the sake of the child.'

'For the sake of the child.'

After dark, when all the cottages looked closed for the night and the villagers asleep, Angus took the cart along the peat track away from the village and out towards the pool by the falls. Night-time had brought a fresh fall of rain and the river was roaring in full spate. He knew the falls would be a torrent, a deafening torrent and that the pool would be deep and flowing.

When the track ended, Angus pulled the hide from the back of the cart and slowly started out across the bog, dragging the skin behind him. As he walked he stumbled in the soft ground sometimes sinking as far down as his waist in moss, and then he'd struggle back to solid ground, feeling the heather brushing his shins once again. He'd find then the fallen faces of old peat banks and jump into their open ground. Some were as old as the village itself, and out beside them were the *feannagan* that sustained earlier settlements and the walls of the spring and summer houses now derelict and redundant.

Angus reached the pool by the falls. In the darkness he could see the torrent of white water falling from its edge into the ink-black pool. He unrolled the hide and laid it flat on the sodden bank of the river. He lay down on its blood-reddened surface and slowly folded the skin around his body until, finally, he pulled the bull's neck and head skin down over his own face and he rolled onto his front closing out the night.

As he lay beside the pool, the roar of the falls grew stronger and stronger in his head. For a while he was aware that he was shivering violently but then the shivering faded into the background of his thoughts and he felt weightless, detached from all things in his surroundings save for the all-consuming roar of the falls.

Angus was then not on the riverbank but in the water. His skin was not bull skin but salmon skin, blue and silver, plated with scales and he was in the pool leaping the falls in a single leap that threw him into the shallows above. He swam on, but not to the spawning ground, not to the gravel of life's beginning and end. He swam up the river as he meandered far inland through pools and falls, dark water and white water. He swam the river until it was no longer water but ice flowing in a glacier from between soaring mountain peaks.

In the shallows of the ice meltwater he placed his back against the air and waited, waited for Osprey to fetch him, waited for the eagle and its claws to take him and carry him to the cave mouth.

In a flash of feathers he was lifted from the water and flew now upwards to the mountains, held in Osprey's claws. Osprey did not speak or sing. Bear was beneath them, Fox was there and Wolf, too. Crow circled, black movement like an eddy in the darkness, but did not come close. It was, knew Angus, to be a safe passage to the spirit of the child.

Soon, after passing the high, sparse birch forest and on into the pines and above to the limit of all growth, the glow of a fire came into view, the glowing pupil of the cave's dark eye, and they went to ground.

Angus walked to the cave mouth and saw the child sitting there, patiently as though it had been waiting for him. Others at that fire looked at Angus and did not fight when he lifted the child and walked from the cave back to the river. What use, they thought, a life taken without knowledge and experience – the child has not used its spirit, the spirit belongs still in the child, and there it will return.

The man lay wrapped in the bull hide at the side of a pool. In the darkness, a shadow moves, steps quietly towards the pool. He stands above Angus, the noise of the falls and the yell of the storm wind hiding his footfalls and his movement in the heather. In the darkness, a sudden glint of silver, a flash of metal upwards with slow deliberation, and then down with reckless force into the centre of the hide. And then the blade is raised again and brought down into the hide, and again and again until the ground is sodden with blood. The man, exhausted with the effort of killing, the effort of forcing through the hide, falls to his knees. Slowly he rolls the body, still in the hide, into the pool and it splashes into the dark water, floats momentarily and sinks; sinks from view.

In the village, a baby coughs and then cries and its mother cries with tears of joy. He is back. He came from far inland.

When all of the stones were gone from those hands and his mouth was full, Sorley leaned over the body and saw that flesh had grown where once there was only bone.

The face he saw was his own face. The hands were his own hands, the redness of the hair his own redness.

He cupped the head in his hands. It was light, as though not human at all. He slowly raised its mouth to his own mouth, parted the lips and closed them on his own and let the stones fall from his own mouth into that he was kissing, and he lay down beside the body.

THREE

'*. . . Fàg mi! Fàg mi!*' Sorley yelled as though he were still under attack. His eyes opened slowly from an unfamiliar darkness to an unfamiliar light and he felt a sudden piercing pain in his eyes as the white neon world came back to him.

Theresa was at his bedside. She held his hands tightly and, half-weeping, half-smiling with relief at his return, she flung her arms around him.

'Sorley, you're going to be all right', she said, repeatedly kissing him about the face. 'Everything's okay.'

Sorley was unable to answer her clearly; his words were stopped by four inches of clear plastic tubing that protruded from his mouth. His arms were bandaged and his hands were pierced with pipes that emerged from under his skin and were bound with sticking plaster.

He had awareness of time having passed but without sound or pictures; taste or touch; an awareness of falling rapidly and then wakening but he knew these memories were only of the last few moments of his unconsciousness. In his mind he was not in a hospital bed in the city with his wife at his side but in that cave near the summit of the mountain where the body of a man was lying.

Theresa calmed him and for a while he drifted back into sleep and when he woke again she was gone, maybe having returned to her work as a nurse in that same hospital.

He lay awake and outside of his room he could hear nurses to-ing and fro-ing. A tea trolley trundled along a corridor, its crockery clattering. He looked up at the sign on the wall above his bed: 'Nil by Mouth'.

A doctor came into the room and looked at the monitor screens beside his bed, but did not speak to the patient whose eyes were fixed upon him. Sorley's head pounded with a ferocious pain and the skin around the tubing itched fiercely.

Later, Theresa returned to the room.

'You've been lying here for a week,' she said. 'I thought I'd lost you.

When the police called at the house there was a terrible rush, I think they thought you hadn't long to live.

'What happened to you, Sorley? I know you can't answer that now, but who would do this to you?'

Sorley looked at Theresa, as confused by the events as she was. He heard her words as she spoke them, but was not listening.

'Danny has been running the shop.' She paused thinking of what to say next, aware that all was small talk in the face of such events.

'Aunt Peigi died and I was at the wake . . .' she said, starting again, desperate to make conversation.

Then Theresa was silent and sat uncomfortably in the chair not knowing what to say to the bruised man in the bed, the mute, half-woken man who lay there.

'They gave me a bag with your things inside it. Blood and guts mostly and a few torn books, soaked and stinking of God knows what,' she began again and hunched a half-smile with her shoulders at her own words.

Sorley did not reply. He turned his face away from her and closed his eyes. He slept but woke when he became aware that Theresa was leaving.

'Theresa,' he said, the tone in his voice asking her to remain, 'something happened to me. I need to tell you what happened to me.'

'Okay,' she replied and sat on the edge of the bed.

'When I was beaten, it must have been when I became unconscious, I felt as though I was flying, leaving the road, flying above the city and away.'

'I'm sure it's just a sensation,' she interjected.

'No,' he replied abruptly, almost as she spoke the words. 'I was flying. I was flying away from the road, and flew miles away, somewhere else.'

Theresa made no comment, aware that Sorley was anxious, disturbed even, by the experiences he had had.

'I came down and was in a small boat in a bay and then flew on to mountains, to a cave.'

He stopped then, as though startled by his own words. But he began again as though remembering details of a dream, details that flashed back to him, triggered by his own words.

'There was a body, just bones in the cave and I sat there beside it and I can remember thinking that the bones were my bones, my own bones without the flesh.'

'Sorley, I think you should try and rest, don't let these things worry you just now, there'll be time when you're better to talk. You've been in a coma, you're bound to be in shock.'

'No, listen,' he replied with energy, as though the story was now becoming clear and fascinating to him rather than frightening.

'Okay, I'm listening,' she said almost sarcastically, but he carried on.

'The bones, the bone hands held stones and I wanted to eat them, I felt I wanted to eat them and I did. I did eat them, one by one and as I ate them I saw and heard stories and then there were people there in the cave. They were my relatives, my old relatives, some I'd never heard of before but my grandmother was there and she knew them. They all knew the stories, they were in the stories, the stories were their stories, things in their lives.' He paused.

'One of them, a boy at first and then a man, could bring back the dead. He would go some place in a trance and I saw him save a child as he had been saved himself. And all of it was on the island, they were at home.' He paused again.

'I think they gave me that gift, I think that is what it was all about, they gave me that gift, they showed it to me. No, that's not it at all, they showed me that I have that gift, and now I'm here, back here in this city. I've had that gift all along, it's been mine and I can think of times – when I was a child – I've used it and didn't know what was happening . . .'

'Well, I'm glad you're back, Sorley,' interjected Theresa.

'As I was in that cave I heard them talking, they spoke in tongues, like animals, like birds or dogs and I knew what they were saying.'

He looked away from Theresa.

'I was happy there. More than happy, I felt euphoric.'

He stopped suddenly as though the word had stalled him, and he was shocked at his own admission.

'Sorley, I think you should stop now. We'll have time to talk all of these things over. It's probably just the dreams of the coma, nothing, nothing to worry about, just things in the mind.'

'I can't think that. It was real, as real as I am in this bed . . .' and then Sorley fell silent and drifted back into sleep.

When he woke, Theresa was gone and he was lonely. He felt alone in the hospital, wounded, isolated, but the memories of the cave, the memory of that specific, new euphoria comforted him – he was chosen, in his generation the gift had fallen to him.

To Sorley, Theresa was beauty as he had always imagined it to be. She had red hair with pale white skin, and a small face that erupted with vigour when she smiled.

They had met in a bar in Glasgow. He was alone, drinking quietly in a corner reading a newspaper when the bar filled with a crowd of women who took seats next to where he was sitting. Half-drunk, the redhead with the green eyes who drank pints of the black stuff had started talking to the man with the paper.

When Sorley told Theresa that he was going home she scrawled her phone number on a ripped shard of beer mat. He pocketed it, kissed her on the cheek and left, thinking that more than likely he would never see her again, bar talk being bar talk.

The following morning he found the scrap of card with the number on it in his pocket, and later that evening called her. Theresa answered the phone. He found himself apologising for calling her, but she said she would like to see him again and so they arranged to meet in the same bar.

Later that week they met, talked and parted, kissing each other lightly on the cheek as they were going, more as though they were siblings than future lovers and it was nearly two weeks until they met again.

All was different then and Sorley knew as soon as Theresa walked into the bar that night that they were going to be lovers. He had gone to order drinks and when he came back she placed her arm lightly around his shoulders, half on the back of the seat as though she still harboured a little reticence towards him.

After a couple of pints the talking stopped and they sat kissing, laughing occasionally at nothing, and then kissing again.

In the following weeks their lives became entwined. Theresa's alternating patterns of shifts at the hospital made the lovers plan ahead, meet at odd times of the day and night. Through it all their attachment to each other grew stronger and they were living together without ever having really made a decision to do so, when events parted them. Early in the morning, the phone rang.

'Jesus,' said Theresa, angered at being woken, 'who the fuck can be calling us just now?'

'I'll go,' replied Sorley, rising sleepily from the bed.

When he returned to the bedroom, Theresa knew that he'd received bad news. Sorley sat silently on the side of the bed.

'It was my brother. I've to go over quickly, to the island. My mother's been taken ill overnight.'

'It's okay, Sorley, go.'

'I've got to . . . I've got to go now, only it's been five years since I was there before.'

Overnight and in the early morning, snow had fallen on the city, quietly and steadily, but out in the Highlands, the snow kept on and was driving hard from a black sky all that day. Flights from the city's airport were delayed and there was not a plane leaving for the island until the following evening.

When he finally made it home he found his mother lying in silence, her skin was ashen and she was unconscious, far off from them all, lost in her final moments. But she did not die then; she stayed with them, living through the silent workings of a machine, living amidst a tangle of wires, almost unrecognisable.

A day became a month and on occasional days she would open her eyes and maybe try to say a word to the anxious faces that peered at her from around the bed. And then, just as they thought she was improving, she slipped away.

Sorley's mother had not known that he had made it back to her bedside. She died, as far as he knew, thinking that he had not come to her. Maybe, he thought, she had decided that he didn't care about her or think of her anymore. He wanted to tell her that he was there, but it was too late. She was beyond hearing, out of touch with them all when he arrived and despite the moments he had taken holding her head, his face close to hers quietly telling her that he was there, he was not sure that she knew it or comprehended who he was or what he was saying.

A minister came to the small hospital room in which they sat, and in which she lay. He muttered some final prayers and then, when it was all over he shook hands with the brothers, offering condolences and asked them to call him to discuss the 'arrangements'.

She died without her husband being with her. Sorley's father couldn't face the end. He was not going to cope with her death, and he had always said that he wished that he would go first. Her death left him forlorn, as though abandoned in a strange land in which the familiar places, the voices and words, had fallen off the edge of the world into the darkness, leaving him without the conversation of their daily lives, without knowing what to eat or drink, how to order life, how to survive all of a sudden as a self-contained, private individual, a widower.

When Sorley and his brothers returned to the cottage that night and told him that she had gone, he sat in silence in his armchair in the kitchen, her chair was opposite him, empty now, but he did not cry. He was quiet and remained so until he too died not a year later. He died, it seemed to those who knew him, having said only a few more words to anyone, consumed with grief and loss and longing.

The day after his mother's death, Sorley had walked to the cemetery to find the grave and to mark out the plot for the gravedigger. The snow had ceased falling and had frozen hard on the machair that covered the shore-side cemetery.

The sky was pink and the snow was laminated with its light, the soft glow of the day. Daylight lasted only five or six hours at that time of the year and the grave would be dug on the morning of the funeral.

The following day they laid her to rest in the dark sand of the cemetery. The family had gathered in the church and when the service was over they gathered again under the midwinter sky, and the distant cry of a curlew went to the graveside with the huddle of mourners.

The funeral passed in the natural silence that is unique to the calm, cold, midwinter days on the island. A wave would break noisily on the shore, carrying with it into the cemetery the sound of the sea. They laid Sorley's mother to rest next to his grandmother in the silence of the dunes, and in the silence of the moorland.

After the burial, their remaining family returned to the family croft house. The small gathering was fed soup and drams by well-meaning neighbours who had rallied to the cause. Hospitality was extended even to those they were suspicious of, those they had forgotten until death had brought them back to mind and the island, and gathered them together in that old house.

The uncomfortable silence of the afternoon was broken only occasionally by one of their number reminiscing about the times the family had spent together in days long since gone, the old days when they lived together on the island.

One cousin recalled from her youth tales of Sorley's great-grandfather whose life story had been a common theme in the ceilidhs that his mother and grandmother had attended.

Sorley's great-grandfather, so the story went, had married on the island but had then, like most of the island men of his generation, taken to the sea and was away from home whaling in the waters of the north Atlantic for stretches of maybe two years at a time.

When he came home, he would speak little of his voyages, but once he spoke of having a new life in a region of the far north east of Canada, a life living among the Inuit folk.

He said they revered – even honoured – his skills as a whale hunter, and they traded furs, guns and even oatmeal with him and the company he worked for. In return, the whalers obtained unhindered use of good, natural, ice-free harbours, and had friendship and shelter on the land in poor weather.

When the whalers arrived each year in the north waters, it was to coincide with the arrival of the migrating whales whose year-round journeying took them thousands of miles from the northern to the southern seas and back again. They returned north each year to spawn and the locations of their spawning grounds were identical, generation after generation.

In the Inuit community that relied on the constancy of the whale migration, and to whom it was like a calendar charting the year and its work, the women of the village played a major, if not as equal a role in the hunt as their menfolk.

The whalers knew that if they befriended the Inuit they would gain their wealth of knowledge, and the hunt would be successful. Many, in their loneliness having spent months or years away from their Scottish homes, married Inuit women, and many had second families, too.

Eventually, rumours started to spread around the island; rumours that were started by the loose-tongued ranting of another whaler who returned home after a long spell at sea and drank himself senseless until he did not know when to stop talking and who told whoever wanted to listen that Sorley's great-grandfather had married an Inuit woman, and he was, therefore, married to two women at once, the Inuit and the Gael. When the rumour reached his own home his island wife confronted him, and he confessed that it was true; he had married again on the far side of the ocean.

So it emerged that the whaler had taken an Inuit wife and had fathered a child and when the story of this new family reached his wife on the island she was devastated but what became of them all at that time is not certain.

Certainly, it was known that the family had left the island for a while, and the croft was shared out between their close relatives while they were away. And it was known that they returned to the croft maybe two years later and with them they brought an Inuit woman and an Inuit child – a girl – who was raised as one of their own family.

Nothing of the small Inuit girl remained now, except these stories. When she came to the island her name was changed to a Gaelic family name and she was christened anew, as though she were a newborn baby.

When the story about the Inuit girl had finished, an elderly neighbour added that his mother too had spoken of these events. She had told him that the Inuit girl and her own children – for she married an island man – were as strange in their behaviour as anyone to whom the village had ever been a home.

They were, he said, only at their happiest when the summer months took them out onto the moors. They would stay at the sheilings for longer than most families, and they would go out to the moors earlier in the year than most other families, too.

Throughout all of this retelling, Sorley's father had sat silently on his own in the small front room of the croft house, and only came into the gathered crowd when he heard what story was being told. He greeted what he heard with a simple put-down: 'Well, we don't talk about that,' he said, 'not today, anyway,' and the story finished.

Before he left the island, Sorley had meant to ask his father to tell him the truth about these stories, but he had not and at his father's death his chance was gone.

⋆ ⋆ ⋆

After his mother's death, Sorley returned to Glasgow and to Theresa and they grew closer then but it was not until he returned to the familiarity of the city that his grief at the loss of his mother found expression. He wept on the night of his return, wept in the darkness of Theresa's bedroom. She cradled him but he could not speak to her of his loss. He thought his grief was indulgent because it was for all the things he had lost at his own hand. He had left the island when he was young and had turned his back on his parents but had never meant to become a stranger.

However, intentions aside, his absence meant that Sorley had become a ghost in the life of his elderly parents. His mother had died knowing nothing of his own life. He was just their son and he had, on reflection, painful as it was, ignored them, taken their existence for granted, and now his mother had gone.

On the night he returned to the city, he woke early in the morning and, as if it were coming from outside his bedroom window that very day, he could hear his father's voice singing the slowly flowing lines of an old Gaelic song.

Sorley had last heard his father singing when, as a boy, the family had made one final summer visit to the moor to stay for a week at the nearly dilapidated sheiling.

One night, as the sun was setting, Sorley heard the sounds of a Gaelic *Salm* rising from close by to his grandparents' sheiling, a little further down the riverbank. The old folk were singing from The Book and the sound of the psalms, with his grandmother giving the response to his grandfather's precenting, blended with the sounds of the river and the sound of birds calling from out on the moor.

When his father and mother heard the psalm they stopped their work preparing for the night but they did not walk to join that congregation at the other sheiling. They stood still where they were, outside by the riverbank and joined the chorus with his grandmother.

The voices and the singing went from his head and Sorley got out of bed and went to the kitchen, where he stood, staring through the window out into the darkness and he recalled the walk he had taken on the moor the day after his mother's burial.

Sorley had walked that day out into the backcountry, up behind the village. He had walked the peat road, stumbling on the loose stones of the rutted track that had been cut in deep grooves by tractors pulling their heavy loads over the soft, shifting surface.

Where the peat road ended, where the road and the river met, he carried on walking, wading through the cold, rushing river water towards the far bank, not resting from his unsteady, tumbling, forward motion until his feet were again on dry land.

Breathless with the pace of walking and the weight of the water on his thighs as he had stumbled across that river, he stopped, gripped by the cold.

A crow glided effortlessly across the sky, cawing at things unseen by Sorley and then it turned towards him and cawed again as though swearing at the stranger on the road before flying, wild with rage at his intrusion, towards the summit of the moorland hills. In moments the bird had disappeared from his view and the moor was silent again.

Struck with rage, Sorley yelled in the direction the bird had flown.

'Fuck you, too!' he shouted at the bird.

'Fuck the lot of you!' he added, gesturing with a single finger.

'Take that,' he said, thrusting his finger upwards, 'to your fucked crow family and shove it where crows don't see the daily light.'

As soon as the words had left his mouth another crow, not seen by Sorley as it lay in a hollow in the snow close by, rose on black wings that shimmered in the faint sunlight and flew low and silently over the heather toward the hills.

It was an omen, he thought, a terrible omen.

Sorley turned and started to walk towards the hills, meandering as he walked around the flooded remains of old peat cuts and the white-green, bulbous humps of moss colonies. In the moor's swampy, brackish pools white tufts of last summer's cotton grass protruded above the snow and blew in the icy breeze like the fragile flames of a thousand birthday candles.

But Sorley had no wish for them, had no desire left in him for anything. He counted the candles. He was by their reckoning one hundred and eighty-nine years old.

'Thank you', he muttered, it's been a lovely day.'

He was addled. Fucked. His mind was destroyed by grief and loss. It was, he thought, too late for him now, a chance at a deeper kind of happiness with love at home and with the love of his parents was gone for good. He was a dead man, a feral man. A man walking out to the place he really belonged: the moorland wilderness, the grand, empty space of his childhood.

'Sorley MacRath – *Fear na Slèibhtean*' it would say on his tombstone. A man more at home in the *airigh* than in the bland white houses that choked the character out of the neighbouring villages, and that is where he would go now. He would walk to the *airigh*; stay there on the moor, hidden from sight. He would come and go like a fox through the black aperture of the *airigh*'s doorway, and he would laugh like a fox too, when he wanted to. No one would hear him out there, hollering at the *fir-chlis* on the moor's cold, diamond-bright nights: not angry but ecstatic, a child again.

From the *airigh* he would fly into the winter night and swoon in the aurora's embrace, her arms swirling about him, the solar wind dusting him. At the *airigh* he would take off his shirt and then tie it to a long stick. He'd climb on the roof and put his new flag there, high above the moor where it would flap in the Arctic gale, a prayer flag for the far north, a perpetual prayer to the beauty of the northern wilderness: the infertile, acidic, moonlit wilderness of the upper globe.

'The weather's been good, considering what the atmosphere's made of,' he said to the crow as it flew into the distance.

He walked on. Before him, a single plover piped a monotonous song, a single tone held for a moment and then dropped and then repeated again.

From the moor, maybe half a mile away, came the faint reply of the plover's mate, and both then sang together, overlapping their tones.

Sorley glimpsed the light brown and white plumage of the plover and saw its black breast. Maybe it was crow underneath, a crow in plover's clothing. He'd known a few like that in his time. The bird stood motionless as he closed on its moss-ball perch. He walked on. The bird's marble eye followed him but it was not the psychopathic eye of the crow. No. The plover's eye was benign, it had John the Baptist's eye, the eye of a martyr alone in the wilderness calling to its mate. Temptation resisted for forty days and forty nights. In its song, the plover pleads for the moor. Good things come from every situation.

Then Sorley looked again and it was not the Baptist's eye that caught his gaze, it was Basho's eye. Plover Basho pinning his one-note poem on the doorway of the wilderness before moving on, further on up the north road leaving behind no trace of its being but its gift.

Sorley walked until he reached the summit of the hill and there, just below the horizon, stood a solitary birch. Sorley walked to it and closed his hands around its narrow trunk. He moved his hands over the coarse, deeply grooved bark until he found the rutted, swollen rims of old cut marks.

His fingers traced the outlines of the words written there in the bark. Letters he had carved himself. His fingers traced the letters of many names, and as he felt the letters so he said the names and the wind carried them over the moor again, over the river and out towards the sea and the distant mountains. As he said those names so he thought again of the dream he had had as a child of their neighbour Calum running out onto the moor, his own mother's sadness at his dream and subsequent trauma and the events that happened soon afterwards.

Sorley recalled the events as though they happened yesterday but other than a foreboding of second sight, their significance was not clear to him.

In the weeks after that dream, he had noticed that the days began to hold a little of the warmth of spring and, as was usual, he walked with his father out to their peat banks to begin that year's cutting. He had taken his fishing rod with him and planned to fish whilst his father marked out the ground for turfing.

Sorley's father started work, scoring the ground the full length of the peat bank and after a few minutes his father, knowing that the boy was keen to get started with his fishing, told him he could head off for the river. Sorley nodded, took up his rod and walked the few hundred yards down the moor from their peats to the edge of the river.

The slow pools that he had left at the end of last summer's fishing were flushed with dark, cold water and where at the end of last season's fishing there had been rocks protruding from the middle of a slow flow, now there was an abundance of white, fast-moving water tinged with the brown of peat sediments washed down from the moors.

Sorley had walked upstream towards the line of big pools close to their neighbour's peats. It was a spot that was once renowned for early salmon, but netting in previous generations had reduced the quantity of big fish going up the river and those pools, far out on the moor as they were, were not now used by the men of the village as their yield had fallen to nothing.

The village boys, who spent half their lives out on this river during the long summer months, would fish there and often, if they were out early in the day, they would catch brownies, or brown trout, bigger than their own feet in those pools, and they would carry them home triumphantly to be gutted and eaten for lunch. The sweet pink flesh was a treat and would be eaten with only a little buttered bread or, as was Sorley's favourite, with hot toast.

Sorley walked towards the pools but even before he had arrived at his favoured spot he saw the tip of a fishing rod protruding over the large outcrop of rocks that formed a slight bend in the river at that point. The rod was held aloft and was motionless, and Sorley could see a clear fishing line stretching back over the waters of the big pool.

Sorley knew it was Calum fishing there and many times in previous summers they had fought over who would get that spot. But he knew that Calum and his father had gone ahead of them on the peat road, and he knew Calum would make straight for their favoured pitch and claim it for the first day's fishing of the year.

For all the big fish they had taken from that pool with its flowing waterfall, which dropped fifteen feet between sharp boulders at its upstream end, it was a difficult pool to fish. The floated line would, if cast into the fast-flowing central stream of the pool, run with the flow to the sea and, where the stream showed the first signs of slowing, the float would turn and begin to slowly drag itself upstream again, working at the edge of the main flow, caught in the forceful undercurrent.

The line floating upstream had, for the first few times Sorley had fished that pool, made him think that he had hooked a big fish which was swimming upstream in an effort to escape capture. Sorley had, those first few times, struck the line only to find that worm and hook were intact.

Sorley sat at the bank of a smaller pool, lower down in the system, and took a large, dark-red worm from the small jar he had all but filled from their garden. He held the worm between his fingers and slowly threaded it over the full length of the new silver hook he had tied on his line.

Slowly, he drew the rod back and flicked the line and float out into the dark water under the far bank where the pool looked deep and calm. Here, he hoped, would be waiting his first hungry fish of the year. The float dragged downstream a little and then remained almost still at the edge of the pool.

He had learnt to be patient, early in the year. The fish were still sluggish in the cold water and they did not lunge at the line as they would in high summer when they were full of life and energy, robust with muscle in the warming river waters teeming with insect life.

Sorley sat in silence and was motionless out of fear that his movement might frighten a fish, and his efforts would be useless. Now and again he glanced over at Calum's rod tip protruding above the rocks and saw that from time to time he too would haul in the line and recast in a short sharp jerk of the tip. Then, barely audible, but clear to those who knew the sound, he would hear the float hitting the water.

He remained sitting in silence. Above him, a large black crow circled its razored caw over the moorland and he saw a pair of great black-backed gulls gliding above the cairn, low over the dark land. But otherwise the moor was still slumbering in its wintered dream, waiting to be woken by the arrival of stonechats, cuckoos and, later, the grating night alarm of the corncrake and the solemn, solitary piping of plovers.

As Sorley sat with time suspended in the reverie that close contact with the river and moor induced in him, it was the force of the breeze, the hush of coarse grass and the flowing water that filled his thoughts.

As he sat there, motionless and almost forgetting that he was fishing, his float was suddenly tugged violently down to the depths of the pool and disappeared for a moment into the brown water before surfacing yards away from its last resting point.

Sorley lifted the tip of the rod and felt the quivering force of the fish he had hooked, which was bending his rod almost in half. The unseen combatant turned once more towards the upstream depths and the line darted again but the fish was tiring and slowly Sorley turned the line onto the spool until at his feet, its pointed head and black-button eye naked in the air, he had a large brown trout. The fish moved wildly in a muscular wriggle and was then still. But as soon as it was still it would struggle again on the riverbank.

The fish flipped and coiled about the line until Sorley took it in his hands and twisted the hook from its mouth and deep red blood flowed from its pink gills and oozed away from the needle-sharp point of the hook and its gripping barb. Gasping and choking it quivered and convulsed in defiant spasms.

Sorley lifted the fish into the air above the nearest rock and swiftly brought its head down with a low thud onto the rock and the muscle froze. The stunned fish went straight, quaking for a second as life struggled in its nerves and then it was rigid, still and cold and moved no more. Sorley looked at its skin, the brown background, lit with a line of red spots and the fine tips, white as his own skin.

Sorley took from his pocket a length of string and threaded the fish through its gills onto a knotted end and hung it from a protruding heather branch high on the riverbank. It dangled heavy on the line and lifted its tail slightly towards the clear sky as the first stiffness of death locked its suppleness.

His day was complete and he could not wait to greet his father with the fish and return home, expectant of the welcome a good fish always received in their house. He could, as expectation filled his mind, smell the fresh stench of the fish's innards as he slowly opened its guts with the point of the old, small kitchen knife with its bright, work-worn blade they always used for gutting fish.

Then, before him, he would see the black-red stomach and the pink, worm-like intestine he'd pull from the gut wall. He'd wash the cavity where the guts had been and then scrape from the exposed white spine the black nerve cords that ran from head to tail.

The fish was then ready and would be coated in flour and oatmeal and eased into a shallow pool of yellow fat, a flood of melted butter, warming in the frying pan.

All present in the house would want a flake of its light pink flesh, but he would get the most and on a good day, with maybe ten fish dangling on the string, he would eat pounds of trout in one sitting.

Occasionally, when the conditions were very favourable and it was easy to predict a good catch, his mother would have a pan of small boiled potatoes ready on his return that would, like the fish, be eaten with the hands.

But such feasts would be the joy of later in the season and now he was grateful for one decent catch so early on in the year. And he thought then of the grace his mother would intone over the fish as he sat at the table, a grace he recalled as being more fully expressed over the food that the moor provided than anything they bought from the small army of travelling vans that toured the outlying villages of the island and brought meat and bread and kitchen goods to these remote houses.

It was as though, unlike the carcasses they hung and slaughtered in the barn or the goods that came in packages from the town, this food came straight from God and was God's providence, and as the hunter he too was being blessed in those solemnly hushed phrases.

As Sorley began to pack away his rod and take down the catch, he looked over to the pool where Calum was fishing. He did not see the tip of Calum's rod above the corner rock and as he climbed the first steps up onto the moor and away from the riverbank he could not see Calum walking towards his father or the family peats.

Sorley stopped and turned back to the river, dropping his line and catch on the dark heather as he walked to the large pool where Calum had been fishing. Expecting to see his friend repairing tackle or unhooking a fish from the line, he jumped with a shout over the last hillock, hiding him from the view of the bank of that large pool.

His feet landed at the top of the heather-capped incline that formed the edge of the bank and Sorley was half-laughing as he anticipated the sudden starting of his friend. But the bank was empty, and the bank opposite, likewise, was empty. At his feet was Calum's rod, its butt close to the water and the float out in the water at the far side of the pool.

Sorley called Calum's name, expecting him to be hiding, having seen his friend approach. But his calls were met only by the sound of the crow cawing and the wind in the coarse grass and the constant roar of the river as it fell over the small falls as it rode down, from pool to pool.

Far off, the calling of the seagulls started again as they soared over the hillside cairn and then there was silence and all was still except for the ragged, jaunty movement of a black tern flying towards the ocean, its body and wings waving like a torn black flag in the breeze.

Sorley noticed that Calum's fishing bag was left open leaning against a rock and he knew then that Calum could not have deserted the spot.

Realising then that the scene was not normal or familiar, that something was very badly wrong, Sorley started to yell Calum's name desperately and started to run back to his father, working at the peat banks. As he approached he could see that other men out on the moor had heard his yelling and all had stopped and were looking at the running boy and his father. Calum's father stood on top of their peat banks and as Sorley neared he dropped his spade and made for the anxious boy.

The men standing and watching from their peat banks saw the boy run into his father's arms and then they saw the father turn and run back to the river with the boy shouting over to his neighbours.

The other men, watching the commotion and hearing the calls for help, now dropped their tools and they too hurried towards the river and the running men and the shaking boy.

At the large pool, Calum's father took off his shirt and vest and dropped slowly into the river, wading into the mouth of the pool. His white torso seemed paler in the open, and his protruding ribs more brittle.

Sorley's father went into the water and the two waded, stumbling on the slimy, rocky bed of the river, blindly feeling below the surface for the missing boy.

Sorley called to them and said that they should search the top of the pool as that was how the current moved and they turned and waded into the deep water until, nearly halfway along, they could wade no further as the pool deepened.

Another neighbour reached the pool, and he, renowned as a good swimmer, removed his coat and shirt and went into the deeper top end of the pool, swimming close to the bottom of the waterfall. To one side of the main flow he took a mouthful of air and went below the rippling current into the still, dark water beneath.

Calum's father was standing shivering in the river and all fell silent and waited, watching where the man had dived in. Seconds passed, each weighing in time more like an hour, and then the man slowly came to the top, gasping and clutching at the elbow the limp body of a boy.

All those at the riverbank then rushed to the bank beside the man and the body of the boy and both were hauled back onto dry ground. Sorley saw that Calum was not moving and was not breathing and his face had turned a pale, cold blue. They laid the drowned boy on his side on the bank and his father frantically pushed at his lungs, expelling small mouthfuls of water from the otherwise motionless head of the boy.

Calum's eyes were open, dark and still, staring blankly like those of the stunned trout. Gazing but not seeing. His skin was pallid. The men lifted him between them and carried him back over the moor and onto the road.

As the men hurried with Calum's body to the outskirts of the village, they could see the women of the village coming up the road to meet them, and one ran faster than the others. It was Calum's mother, wailing at the sight of her child being borne home motionless in the arms of the village men, his hair dripping wet and his limbs loose at his side.

They laid him on the ground before the croft house and a doctor came and broke into the huddle of men. His father was frantically pumping at the boy's lungs, trying to push out the river water and, with tears running down his face, he placed his head against the boy's naked chest. But he did not hear a heartbeat and he closed his eyes and sobbed tears that ran across the boy's skin.

The doctor lifted the man from the body and checked the boy for a pulse. Turning to face them, he shook his head and the mother fainted into the arms of the gathered crowd. Sorley's father took off his jacket and placed it over the face of the drowned boy.

Sorley turned to his mother.

'I told you this would happen, I told you,' he said, and when the realisation of what he had said hit his mother, she let out a low scream, a scream of sickness rather than terror.

Sorley turned and ran from the sobbing huddle. He ran onto the peat road, not stopping as his lungs heaved for air and his tears salted the corner of his panting mouth.

He turned and saw the huddle in the village and heard their crying, not stopping until he was by the peat banks where the discarded spades and jackets still lay.

He ran towards the river's roar and he found lying there, facing the sky with his pale blue eyes open and still beneath a run of river water, the body of the drowned boy. His hands were clenched in their dying fist, his fingers reddened with blood from where he had taken hold, in vain, of the jagged, weed-washed stones on that riverbed.

In his closed hands he held silt from that riverbed and his eyes glinted with the silver of river grit.

Sorley took a handful of the silt and held it, until it was again an ice flow, flowing from a glacier, far inland, and the boy was carried on as it journeyed to the sea.

Sorley held the river silt until it was a black stone and the darkness of the day was furled in his hand. Sorley held the black stone until it was white quartz and he placed the white stone on the open eye of the boy.

He watched as the boy's body drifted to the sea and when it was gone from his sight he turned and walked slowly to the point on the moor where there stood a solitary birch tree. Calum was there at the tree. Crow and buzzard circled high above but neither spoke. Sorley saw Calum and asked him to come back, and he nodded and was gone.

Taking from his pocket a sharp stone he had held at the riverbank, Sorley began to carve letters into the bark.

The name of the drowned boy.

The names of those who had gone before.

The names of the past.

The names of those who are gone but are not forgotten.

In the village, the body of the boy had been moved to his own bed and had been dressed ready for the wake as mourners gathered. The minister was in the main room of the cottage precenting *Salm XXIII – 'Is a Dia fèin a's buachail dhomh'*, to the tune of Crimond . . .

> *Is a Dia fèin a's buachail dhomh,*
> *cha bhi mi an an dìth.*
> *Bheir e fainear gu-n luidhinn sios*
> *air cluainibh glas' le sìth:*
> *'Us fòs ri taobh nan aimhnichean*
> *'thèid seachd sios gu mall,*

A ta e 'g a mo threòrachadh,
gu min réidh anns gach ball.

. . . when the drowned boy convulsed and air spluttered from his mouth.

'He's alive,' his father exclaimed, `he's alive.' He pulled the cloth from the boy's face. Calum's eyes were open and his father held him as his mother and the mourners began to weep, and the minister and men gathered in that room continued the *Salm*.

Sorley recalled how, as darkness fell that day and not knowing of Calum's revival, he had turned and walked back to the village. He knew his mother would scold him and how he had brought shame on them again.

Unseen by other villagers he crept back to the house and as he lifted the latch on the door he looked over at Calum's house, expecting to see it only in darkness, but lights were on and the doctor's car was parked at the front.

As he entered his house, his mother had come to him, neither spoke and she placed her arms around him.

'Calum is alive. He's poorly but alive,' she said, hugging the child and he made no reply, stunned as he was by her words.

Then he was back in the darkness of the city morning, standing in Theresa's flat peering at nothing, fixed in a daydream, hearing his father singing the words of the *Salm* at the *airigh*, out on the moorland.

'What's wrong, Sorley?' Theresa asked.

'Nothing. It's nothing. It's just the *cianalas*, I suppose, the homesickness,' he replied, turning to face her.

'When I was sixteen, I left the island for the first time and went with the other boys of the district on a trip to the Big City,' he said.

'The mother didn't want me to go, but we had decided, all of us, that nothing would stop us and away we went. The father gave me a roll of notes as I was leaving and said "you go and enjoy yourself, son" in a whisper so that mother couldn't hear him.

'Well, with all the other boys I started to drink on the morning ferry, and when we reached the city we drank again in The Park Bar – the mythic Park! How many island men have placated their mothers by saying that when they were away working in Glasgow they only ever met their friends in The Park? And their mothers had said how nice it was that they stayed together, and wasn't a nightly trip to the park a good, clean way of socialising.

'Here we were now, in The Park, it was our turn and we stood there nodding to the island men we half-recognised, speaking English to be big and modern. We drank hard, drams and pints, and left the bar before midnight and found our way to a cheap curry house.

'And weren't we quite the thing? Eh? Drunk and loud and not like island boys at all, and do you know not one of us could even break a poppadom without first feeling compelled to say the Grace and that fell to me. So, with waiters and the strumming of the sitar as my only accompaniment I began to say the Grace in Gaelic.

'But we knew, all of us, that we would always be strangers in the city. We would always be island boys.

'We walked back to the squalid B&B we'd taken at the far end of Sauchiehall Street, rolling on drunken legs as we went, and saying in imitation of our parents that we were all *Breabadair Diluain*. It was the worst punishment you could get, a punishment deferred that could not be given out on a Sunday because the Sabbath law forbade it. I suppose I've carried that with me all my life since then, since leaving the island, a deferred guilt. The pain put off until another, better time when it would be all the more terrible, and I think that time has come.'

Sorley was discharged from hospital into Theresa's care and he stayed in the flat, living almost as a recluse at first, too frightened of the street to walk about alone, and too bruised to show his face.

He sat at home reading, ploughing through the mound of titles he'd accumulated over the years, books he loved for a day or so and then discarded promising himself that he would return to them one day and read them in full. None of his books he could ever dispose of. He bought most of them in bags and boxes over the counter of his shop from strangers wanting only a few pounds in return, some he bought because he thought they would sell well, others simply because he liked the titles, and some because he felt some pity for the seller. All the time he lived hoping that the next big sale would arrive, some obscure title that had a market, maybe abroad, and which would bring in hundreds or even thousands of pounds.

He had not been to the shop since the day of the attack. He could not face walking those familiar streets, maybe even chancing seeing his attacker. The man's face was not clear to him but he knew that he would recognise something about him if he ever did see him again.

Despite Theresa's reassurance, Sorley was not sure if Danny had kept the shop open. He doubted that he had, and Sorley knew that soon he would have to go back to work, but not now, not until the scars had healed and the memories of the attack were less immediate in his mind.

Theresa's sister, Grace, had married Danny apparently on the rebound. She was nearly twenty years his junior and the survival of their relationship had surprised everyone who knew them, except Sorley.

Sorley had seen a kind of childish neediness in Grace from the moment they first met. Her falling for and her engagement to a man old enough to be her father came as no surprise to him. He was glad, in truth, because he knew that she would be happy and the relationship was built on something deep-seated in both of their psyches.

Danny was rugged, thickset but with a gaunt, even bony face that carried a red, wire-haired beard. He was a quiet man who you could be forgiven for thinking of as being 'steady', but in truth both his quietness and steadiness were life-learnt artefacts that shored up a deeper fixation with sorrow and solitude.

Danny came from the northernmost parts of the coast of Argyll and the sea and mountains were strong elements of his being. He was comfortable in the remoteness that both could offer and spent many days in all seasons walking the hills, often alone. His introspection had attracted Sorley and there had always been a strong bond between the two of them.

Danny said, whenever the subject came up in conversation, that climbing and walking in remote corners was a way of meditating, a slow, solitary, repetitive act that induced a kind of focused trance enhanced by the wild beauty of the landscape. And so he would walk until his mind was free but Sorley knew that Danny found comfort in the hills for when Grace had met him, although many years had passed since his wife passed away, Danny was still in mourning, a mourning that was cast in the lead of introspection; a mourning whose weight and density destroyed both words and speech, and so the heights offered solitude, thinking space, clear space and a return to the places where Danny had loved to be with his first love.

Grace could never understand Danny's desire to return to the places he had been with his wife, the landscapes they'd shared together. To her it was contrary to the innate intuitions of emotion, an action that provoked sorrow rather than healing, perhaps a difference between men and women.

Sorley had at first underestimated Danny; his quietness and the precise, almost tutored or mannered exaction of his speech were difficult at times to fathom and easily misunderstood, suggesting an aloofness or indifference to others.

But one night, when the two had gone for a drink to MacFarlane's Lounge, the bar they favoured close to the bookshop, Danny told Sorley of an episode that occurred some years after his first wife had died and he bought a home in a glen they had often visited together.

In its telling, Sorley heard in Danny's voice a tone of acceptance if not resignation to the profundity of loss that overshadows life but also some sense of an opening, a calm resignation, a calm acceptance, a foundation stone for endurance, and in that voice Sorley felt shame at his own weakness, his own inability to endure such loss and how that had led him from place to place, possessing the urge to leave all behind and run from sorrow.

Danny's strength could be his strength. Could he learn to live with the gift that Danny seemed to possess in abundance; the gift of acceptance, of endurance, the gift, perhaps, of humanity? Was not all his dalliance with the second sight, with the supernatural, simply a means of trying to take control over the immutable forces of fallibility when true strength comes from endurance, insight and acceptance of the unchangeable?

'I remember sitting by the fire one Hogmanay night at home,' began Danny that night in the bar, speaking as he always did when he spoke about himself, in a quiet and more reflective voice than usual, 'I was watching the hands of the clock slowly joining at the top. My neighbour, Davy, and myself had seen in the New Year together every year since I moved into that glen.

'Davy was then two years without his wife, Agnes, and although we had kept on with the Hogmanay gathering after she had gone, it had changed. She used to welcome all who wanted to join us and then it became just two lonely men.

'Agnes had died,' explained Danny, 'not suddenly but slowly . . . a withering fade from life that drained Davy of his energy, and aged him. Davy had nursed her at home and Danny had visited her almost every day until she could no longer bear to allow anyone to see her.

'When I left that cottage one day,' said Danny, 'I did not know that that was the last time I would see Agnes alive, but I realised afterwards that she herself had known that to be the case. She said to me how grateful she and Davy were for my friendship, and it comforted her, she said, to think that I would be there to help her husband when she had gone. And I had thought nothing of it, as her farewells were always sad and lingering at that time.

'I went in the following day and Davy stopped me in the sitting room. Agnes can't see you, he had said, she cannot see you anymore. I mean she won't see anybody anymore. It's become too difficult for her.

'Aye, all right, I said, that's okay, but will you tell her that I was in, asking after her? I will, Davy had replied and he said that he didn't think it would be long now; the pain was getting too much for her. And all I could say was sorry, that I was sorry to hear that. I left then, I did not want the old man to see me upset but in truth I was. The fact that she was still there, alive in the next room but in a sense gone, had struck me down with grief.'

Danny stopped then for a moment and drank down the dram he had been rolling in the glass he held before him all the while he had been telling the story. They sat in silence before Danny spoke again.

'It was funny but I could relate to it. Agnes did not want to die away from that glen, and she did not. I remember one night seeing that their porch light was on, and then came the nurse and the doctor. I watched the comings and goings on the glen road that night, the headlights of cars going up and down. I watched at the curtain, waiting for a sign that all was either well, or that it was over for Agnes. And as I watched, my eyes focused on the darkness and I was again at my own wife's bedside as she faded.'

Danny stopped again and shook his head, bringing his hand up to cover his mouth. He breathed in deeply and with a slight shudder in his breath before he spoke again.

'I always thought I'd be strong for Davy when Agnes was dying but that night I was not, I was unable to go and be with him until I finally forced myself to his door. It was open and Davy was sitting alone in the room, awkward in the chair. From the bedroom came hushed sounds, busy sounds, of work not for the living but the dead.

'She's gone, Davy said to me, she's gone and then he began to weep and he wept with his entire body, and all I could do was just sit in the chair opposite him.

'We buried Agnes in the small cemetery that was at the end of the glen. I remember that it was ringed with tall, red-barked pines and firs. The service was held in the glen church that had sat empty, its doors locked, for over a year. The minister spoke of Agnes's goodness and of her hard work. She was, he said, one of the last women to work in forestry in that part of Scotland.

'We hardly spoke of her after she died. The pain left in the old man's heart was too much for words. Davy asked me once how I had coped with the loss of my own wife.

'I haven't, I told him, I don't think you ever do.

'All I could think of was the first time I drove that glen road with my wife. The rain was pouring that day, pouring from a thick grey sky. The mountaintops were not visible from the road but their lower slopes were draped in squalls and we had seen the rising, bell-shouldered rocks of the mountains. They were striated with running water and rowans grew haphazardly in the soil high up, clinging to crevices, impossible you'd think.

'I had driven, I thought, not to the Highlands but to some other place, maybe even Mount Fuji the way you see it in pictures.

'When I last lived in the city,' Danny continued, growing more agitated and lost in his memories, 'I wanted those winter mornings of the glen, the distant views of snow-clad summits. I wanted the sound of meltwater, clear and cold, running rapidly in steep burns to be about me and to feel the wind in my face.'

Danny stopped talking then and did not say any more that night or since about the glen, and Sorley knew then why he returned to those places, why he longed for them like he longed for his wife. It was love, deep and profound and deeper and more lasting he thought than he would ever be capable of himself.

As Sorley thought of the bookshop and Danny so his mind turned to the bag of his belongings that Theresa had brought home from the hospital. He went into the hallway and found it hanging on a peg among the coats they piled onto those few hooks that hung behind the front door.

The bag was made of clear plastic and carried the name of the hospital printed on the side. Inside, as though medical specimens themselves, the books he'd had with him on the night of the attack were individually packaged in sealed bags. He took them out, opened the bags and examined them. Of the four, three were torn and the page corners swollen, crinkled and gummed with exposure to moisture. The other was in worse condition and had acquired an odour unlike any he'd encountered before from an old book.

That night, Sorley went to bed before Theresa had returned home from work at the end of her shift in the hospital. He lay awake reading the old book, its stench filling the room, until the heaviness of his eyes became too much for him and he fell asleep, the book dropping over his face.

Sorley was deeply asleep when a clattering came from outside which woke him with a start and he sat bolt upright in the bed throwing the book to the ground. He went to the window. He looked down at the mess of bins and rubbish on the green behind the tenement; a fox was ripping at a rubbish bag. The fox turned its face and looked up at the man staring down from the window. Their eyes engaged momentarily in a fixed stare and Sorley could feel his heart beginning to race, and for the first time since waking in the hospital he felt elated.

Sorley pressed his face against the glass to see the fox more clearly. The fox barked and in its growl Sorley heard it say his name, and in that moment fear gripped him and he grasped the open curtains, pulling them closed. His heart pounding in his chest he rested his forehead on the closed curtains and drew in deep, gulping breaths.

The sound of the fox's voice ran through his head again and again but it was not the coarse voice of the growl but a softer voice and anger suddenly filled Sorley's head. He opened the curtains once more with a violent pull and threw open the window, leaned out and yelled down at the spot where the fox had been. Sorley became aware that he was not yelling obscenities but howling and barking like the fox as though the animal possessed his voice.

The anger in him subsided. He slowly closed the window and the curtains, disappointed that the fox had fled and that he had not had the courage to remain looking and listening to it when it had first spoken to him.

He went back to bed and as he lay there he could hear the fox's guttural howl coming from afar; coming from a place he imagined to be by the banks of the river that ran along a deep wooded gorge through the outer ring of the city centre. And it was not yelping he heard but words, fearful words; a swollen stream of words that came at him through the darkness.

Sorley closed his eyes. He hoped that sleep would free him from the fox and his thoughts of the cave. He hoped he would sleep and then wake hours later and that the episode was simply imagined, a dream, a mirage, a game played by his mind on his overactive imagination. But in another part of his mind the ecstatic joy of the cave began to grow once more. His heartbeat quickened and his breathing became shorter and shorter. He could feel his pulse pounding in his feet and ankles. He got out of the bed again and opened the front door of the flat. He stood at the bottom of the winding tenement stairway and looked up through its open centre as it spiralled towards the upper floors and Sorley saw that that night the roof of the tenement was missing from above the stairway and he could see the clear night sky.

He flew from the ground, feeling as though the muscular wings of his first flight to the cave were once more on his back, and he went up through the open stone stairway and out through the open roof. The night air was cold and as he flew out over the city he saw the fox and it ran along the banks of the river, keeping with him as he went north. In the distance, Sorley could see the peaks of mountains, their snow-capped summits glowing white in the darkness.

As he flew through the sky he saw something moving rapidly towards him, it was black such that its movements in the dark sky looked as though the blackness of the sky itself was rippling. The fox growled at the shape. The outline grew into that of a bird, a large crow, and it came at Sorley with its claws open. Sorley covered his face as the crow attacked him, its claws cutting deep into his arm and then Sorley and the crow were on the ground. The fox leapt at the bird and bit deeply into its back, pulling it away from Sorley and tearing at its flesh and feathers until its blood ran freely on the ground.

In the struggle before its death the crow stabbed at the fox with its beak and cut deep into its heart.

When the crow lay dead on the ground the fox began to dig into the earth. As it dug blood ran from its wound, a dark crimson red on its brown fur. The fox dug deep into the ground and slowly disappeared into the dark hole of its new burrow. The fox called out to Sorley, called to him from under the earth and Sorley and the fox lay side by side. The ground was cold and snow fell and drifted its flakes slowly into the mouth of the burrow.

When daylight broke, Sorley saw that the fox was dead. He took its body from the burrow and raised it to the heat of the sun before returning it to the ground and closing off the burial place.

Sorley woke as though from a nightmare but he stayed in the realm of that dream, unsure where he was and shivering. Was he underground with the fox or in the remote, snow-covered place where the fox died and lay buried? No, he was in bed and Theresa was at his side, asleep. It was still dark. In his sleep he had seen the fox again and it was talking to him from beyond its grave, sitting beside its own bare bones as he had sat beside his in the cave and he thought then that surely nothing dies.

Theresa woke Sorley later that morning.

'When I came in last night the front door was wide open', she said to him.

'Sorry, did I forget to lock it?'

Theresa did not answer.

'It has happened again.'

'What?'

'Last night, I flew away again, left here and followed a fox from the bins out into the open country. It happened without me thinking about it, it just happened. One minute I was here, in this room, the next I'm out in the hall and going out through the roof. The fox guided me on and we were attacked by a crow, a big black fucking crow that nearly killed me and certainly got the fox.'

Theresa looked at him. He could see in her eyes that she thought he was mad, deluded mad.

'I know you don't believe me, I have trouble myself.'

'I do and don't believe you. I know that you've been very unwell and recovering from a coma and things will be going on in your mind, things that will take time to heal.'

'Yes, that's it. I'm just nuts. None of it's true at all. I'm just crazy, a headcase. Well, I can tell you that it is true. It's all true.'

Theresa was not listening. She turned on her side, her back to him and slept.

Later that morning Sorley came down from the bedroom where he had stayed for maybe three hours reading the old books. Theresa greeted him.

'How are you feeling now?' she asked.

'I'm fine, just fine. I'm going to the shop,' he replied with an edge of stress in his voice as though accusing her of stopping him from leaving.

'Fine,' she replied.

'Danny has kept it going, but nothing much in the away of sales.'

'No. I don't expect so. What's wrong, Sorley?,' she asked him, trying to tackle the tension in his voice. 'I'm going nuts sitting in here, I need to get out, get back to normal, get back to work.'

'Is that all? I mean, is there anything else?'

'Aye, that's all.'

Sorley went to the hallway and the bulk of coats on the hooks. On the wall by the front door was a mirror and Sorley caught a glimpse of his face as he reached for his jacket.

He left the jacket and turned to face the mirror. In the cold grey light of the morning that drenched the old-fashioned painted and tiled interior of that space with the feeling of a kind of melancholic but logical truth, his face was ashen but bleached with pale yellow from the bruising. His left eye was more bloodshot than his right and his cheekbone was swollen. He looked away, determined not to let the sight of his face deter him from moving on.

He put on his jacket and went to the small hall cupboard looking for a bag for the books. The cupboard was cluttered with the usual contents: a vacuum cleaner, tins of household cleaners and a few, small, unpacked boxes from the time he had moved in with Theresa.

He turned the light on and could feel the bright, burning heat of the bulb close to his face as his hands searched before him in the mound of coats and bags and unwanted things stacked there. As he did so he saw at the back of the cupboard the coat he had worn throughout his college days, a full-length leather army officer's greatcoat, its tan colour scratched through years of wear. It had a sturdy, impenetrable quality and in his depressed and agitated mood the security of its thick layer appealed to him. He pulled it out from the cupboard, took off his jacket and put it on. The leather was stiff and near to cracking but the coat fitted.

He turned up its rigid collar and he could feel the thick leather hard against the back of his head. He felt safe then, the coat was awkward and heavy but just wearing it was a comfort and for a second he was again Sorley MacRath, the punk, the Gaelic punk, the confident even arty lad he had been when he moved to the city, freeing himself of the island and the strictures he saw in the lives of its people. He liked himself back then. He liked being confident for the first time in his life. He liked being with other young confident, even arrogant, students: invincible, living away from home almost as though newborn.

He went to Theresa.

'What do you think?' he asked her.

'Crazy,' she replied.

'Well, without the beating and a month in the bed, I'd never have been able to fit back in this coat,' he said, happier than before. 'It's been great for the diet.'

Sorley left the flat with the books in a bag tucked under his arm and walked towards the railway station to catch the train that would take him back to his old life, the bookshop and normality.

The streets were busy with people and as he walked he felt a growing sense that the people that passed him on those familiar streets were looking at him, at his bruised face and bloodied eye, or maybe it was the coat they were looking at. He became self-conscious of his looks and was aware that he was turning his head away from those who walked towards him.

The train was busy, too, and he was forced to stand as it slowly made its way from station to station, passing wooded sidings with steep banks overhung by the walls of houses and factories such that by the time the train was nearing the city centre it was almost underground save for the narrow slit of daylight immediately above the rails.

He left the station and began the walk to the shop. The route would inevitably take him along the road where he was beaten, past the spot where he had slumped unconscious on the road and from where the strange flight had first taken place.

The street was empty as he rounded the corner. He stopped. He had never thought before of its length, was it a mile, a half mile, a quarter mile? It seemed narrower than last time and cluttered with the shadowed openings of the back lanes. He walked on, nervous and saw before him the place where he had been assaulted. He stood looking at that spot. No trace or mark of what had taken place there remained. He turned and looked back down the street in the direction he had seen his assailant stumbling away in the darkness. Walking up the road, he saw the figure of a man, a stranger. His heart started pounding. Was it his attacker? The man walked past not looking at him.

The return to the street and the shop had been a mistake. He was not ready to face it all again. It was trauma, yes, trauma. He was traumatised and could not cope with the reminder of what had happened. But then he was calm again as he thought of the distant mountains and forests far inland, the landscape that had opened to him that night and with it the stones and their stories. He stood at that spot on the road and smiled to himself aware that he was, in fact, nearly laughing with joy.

Another stranger passed him as he stood there and looked hard into his face as though accusing him of insanity.

Sorley walked on a few paces but could not bring himself to return to the shop. Ahead of him he saw the bar, MacFarlane's, that he used for lunch on quiet days when trade was slow.

He went towards it and pushed on its sprung doors expecting to be greeted by the familiar faces behind the bar but all he saw was a face he had not seen before, a young woman behind the bar who did not know him. He looked about the public bar, one or two were sitting there that he half-recognised but who showed no obvious sign of knowing him. Sorley sat on a stool by the bar and ordered his usual lunchtime drink, a half-pint of Guinness and a double Jameson's.

The black liquid in the half-pint glass tasted bitter, disgusting even, the whisky was coarse-edged and fiery and he calmed it with a little water from a jug. He downed the dram and ordered another, keeping the half-pint ticking over slowly as he got through the spirits. It was a bad habit. He looked at the clock after he'd taken his second drink: its hands read two o'clock. He'd go on to the bookshop in an hour, he thought, when the drink had given him some courage because he could not face the road again alone.

He did not, that afternoon, speak to anybody else in that bar. After a couple of drinks he moved to a seat in the corner of the bar and sat reading the old book.

It was the second volume in a series but the opening papers were gummed together by the soaking they had taken on the night of his attack and he did not want to force or tear them apart before he knew if the title had any value and might be worth restoring. The embossed letters on the book's spine simply read 'Rasmussen', and he had reason to think that it had been rebound by one of its previous owners.

At three o'clock he put back the trip to the bookshop by another hour. The drink had warmed him and he had become comfortable in the bar.

At five o'clock the bar began to fill with the usual mix of low-grade office workers in suits who dropped by after work, had a few quick drinks and left. Some stayed longer, unable to pull themselves away from the bar, unable to face the suburban trains.

By six o'clock, Sorley was feeling drunk. His head was beginning to spin and he wanted to leave. He was feeling unsteady on his feet and the drink was making him feel nauseous. He downed a final double and left, heading straight for the train.

Darkness was closing in on the city as his train pulled away from the platform and the carriage he was in was nearly full with commuters.

He had a seat but left it to stand at the doorway, fearful that he might sleep and miss his stop. He looked out of the window and recognised the houses and small industrial units that meant he was nearing his own station.

As the train began to slow, he saw the red fur of an animal lying beside the track. In that fleeting second as the train passed, he saw it lying on its side, its eyes were open, but the fox was motionless. It must have been struck, he figured, as it crossed the tracks, and he saw it in his mind, staring bewilderedly into the approaching train lights before it was killed.

The train pulled slowly into the station and stopped. The doors opened and Sorley stepped out. He took the few steps across the narrow platform and leaned against the brick wall that ran the full length of the platform on that side of the station. With the train pulling out of the station he vomited, two, maybe three, times.

His head cleared and within a few steps he was feeling better, even sober. But, as he walked away, he knew that he could not leave the fox behind on the railway banks. It seemed naked, open to countless thousands of prying, passing eyes.

He made it back to the tenement but did not take the spiral steps to their flat. He walked instead through the close and out the back door to where the residents' sheds and dustbins were located around the small drying green. He went to their own shed, and in the near-darkness of its interior, found a torch and a spade and placed them in an old holdall they had left there when it was too ragged to be used for shopping or travel.

He started back to the station clutching the goods he had taken from the shed and as he reached the platform he climbed down onto the trackside and started to walk back to where the animal lay. He walked back nearly a mile along the track, stepping urgently onto the bracken-covered banks whenever the commuter trains came towards him on their tracks. He came across the body of the fox.

He took the spade and torch from the holdall and started to dig in the rough scrubland beside the track. As he dug, he was gripped by fear, not of the closeness of the passing trains but because he was aware of being watched in the darkness. He was being studied by something that was startled by his actions and his sudden arrival on that scene but he carried on digging until he had made a hole big enough to take the body of the animal. He lifted the fox into the hole so that its head was facing north, because, for some reason, he thought that was right.

Finally, his work completed and the body of the fox covered, Sorley marked the fence next to the spot with a black cross from the soot on the end of a half-burnt stick he found close by.

Fear took hold in him again, a blind panicky fear and he turned and ran from the scene of the burial. He was running and his heart was pounding but he did not know why he was so frightened. His limbs ached and he was forced to stop and rest before he reached the station platform. He vomited again and as his head hung down he thought that his fear was of himself, of his own actions, of his insanity.

Sorley returned to the flat. He was too exhausted and too frightened of the dark that night to return the bag and its contents to the shed at the rear of the tenement, and instead he placed it behind the bulk of shoes and old jackets that had accumulated behind the front door.

Theresa had not returned from work. He undressed in the dark and got into their bed. He was asleep within a few moments.

When he woke, Theresa was by his side in the bed. He had not heard her arrive back from work or felt her get into the bed. It was nearly eleven in the morning, he had slept for over twelve hours and had, for the first time since the beating, slept without the torture of flashbacks, or the half-awake fear of the darkness in the room, or noises on the street outside.

Theresa turned to him, resting on her elbow as she always did when she was unsure of him, or unhappy in some way.

'You stayed out yesterday . . .'

'I had a few drinks, I was in MacFarlane's.'

'Christ, what did you go to that dump for?'

'I was back about seven,' Sorley replied indifferently.

'I called you after that and there was nobody in.'

'You must have called the wrong number; I was here after that, all night on my own. Nobody called me, but then who does now?'

'I do.'

'Well, you didn't last night . . . what does it matter anyway? Maybe

I was having a wash or a shit when you called, I don't know.' Sorley always swore or used foul language to her whenever he was irritated or annoyed with her insistent conversational cross-examination, and she knew, as well, that he swore when he was lying.

'I called again at eight, and there was no answer then either,' she said.

'I went to bed about then.'

'That was early for you.'

'I know, I was tired. What is all this? Where do you think I was? Next door shagging Mrs O'Hara, while Mr O'Hara was out getting a fish supper for us all?'

'You're not supposed to be drinking.'

'Well, I can't help it; I can't stay in here all day and all fucking night alone. I need to get out.'

'Couldn't you wait until I wasn't working and we could go out together for once, instead of you going out again on your own?'

'Why can't I go out on my own? Are you scared that I'll talk myself into another seeing to? Is that it?'

'Okay, I was only asking you. I was only trying to make sure, that's all, and you must look after yourself now.'

Theresa got out of the bed quickly and kept her back to him as she did whenever she was angry with him. She put on the blue dressing-gown he had bought her last year, which she had worn every night and morning since, and went out of the room. The flat was silent then except for the sound of cups and the kettle heating on a cooker ring.

Sorley lay there; the grey light of morning was coming in through the pale blue curtains that were drawn across the bay window that faced north from the flat. He thought of the night before, vomiting on the platform, walking the track, burying the fox, running home. Leaving the bag close to the door.

He thought of the terror he felt on picking up the fox from the track-side, the feeling of eyes looking at him from the darkness, the feeling of something far off observing him from the dark sky. He could see again the body of the fox slowly disappearing beneath shovels of soil, the head going beneath the ground, closing and levelling the shallow grave he had made for it in that fear-filled darkness.

But he knew that it was buried now, safe from any further abuse or violence. It was lying still, its legs stretched as though caught in one final giant stride, one final attempt to escape the approaching lights that finally caught it, crushed it and flung it aside.

He thought of the fox's body lying on the shore beneath the apex of a whalebone arch, its dark eye reflecting the thousand stars of the Milky Way that flowed as if they were the boulders in a mighty, ancient river forging a deep white gorge across the landscape of the sky.

He felt then the open ribs of the wooden boat against his bare skin and could hear the lapping of waves. But this time he was not coming into the bay but was slowly being drawn away from it. Away from where the fox lay in the bone arch. Then the waves were still and night had given way to day again.

While he had been distracted by his thoughts he did not notice that Theresa had returned to the room with two cups of tea and was standing in the doorway looking at him.

'What were you thinking about then, you looked miles away?'

'Last night.'

'Sorley,' she said more firmly, 'what's that bag and shovel doing behind the door?'

Sorley was silent for a second, trying not to show his fear at her question.

'I took a few things with me when I went out.'

'Why did you take a spade to the pub with you?'

'I didn't. I came back and got it.'

'Why? You didn't used to take a spade with you to the sitting room,' said Theresa with a sarcastic half-smile on her face.

'I didn't take it with me, I came back and got it after I had left town.'

'Were you digging the garden when I phoned you then?

'No. I was burying a fox.'

'What? You were burying a fox, a flying fox, I take it?'

'Yes, I was burying a fox, a dead fox I saw by the rail track as I came home. I walked back to it and buried it and then came home again.'

'Are you serious, Sorley?'

'I saw it from the train and I didn't feel as though I could leave it there. It looked naked, it reminded me of what it was like lying in the gutter.'

'Remind me of this again. You came home drunk, got a spade out of the shed and went back down the railway track and buried a dead fox. And then what? What did you do after that?'

'Nothing. I came back here and went to bed, that's all.'

'Are you fucking mad, Sorley? What are you doing going out in the dark burying animals – you could have been hit by a train.'

'I had to, I just had to. I couldn't leave it there. I didn't want you to know . . . but I just had to do it.'

'I don't understand you, Sorley. You should stay in and stay off the drink until your head's straightened out.'

'My head is straightened out. I feel more straightened out now than I have for years. The problem is that you don't like it.'

'How could I like it? You go out to work one day, get drunk and beaten up and spend a month in hospital unconscious. I loved sitting at your bedside watching you breathing through a tube. Then you go out again, barely a month later, and tell me you had to go out and bury a fox by the railway in the darkness. That's just fucking great, Sorley. I feel that everything's really straight now. That's all okay, everything's normal again.'

Sorley got out of bed and walked past Theresa towards the door.

'Well, if you can't see it as being all right, that's not my problem. I feel fine, and that's what I call okay. That is all right behaviour for me.'

One afternoon towards the middle of winter, some four months after he had buried the fox and when Theresa was working nights again, Sorley stood looking out of the window towards the green. They had not spoken of the fox since the day they had argued but Sorley knew from that day that he would eventually have to return to the site of the grave. He would go back for the fox and bring it home. He would uncover it again when nature had cleaned it of its dead flesh. It was meant to be with him.

That night, Sorley returned to the place beside the railway track where he had buried the fox. Guided by the still visible black soot mark on the fence post nearby, he began to open the now overgrown grave of the fox.

As he dug into the familiar, burnt-black soil of the trackside he gradually began to find the coarse, matted, red hair of the fox and green-white fragments of spine showing beneath.

The frail, damp spine was shaped now in a slight curve, the back and front legs reaching for each other as though, after it had been buried, the fox had tried once more to run clear of the train.

With the same fear, the same sense of being watched from the shadows, Sorley dug deeper into the soil and found the small bones of the fox's tail stump. He worked at the other end but the head seemed to be missing from the shallow grave, absent from the rest of the buried carcass. Eventually, by widening the site of the exhumation, he found the head lying maybe a foot from the neck.

The skull was brown except for the last dark fragments of its black lips that clung around the mouth. He lifted the skull from the open grave. The fox's loose teeth fell to the ground and he gathered them hurriedly and pocketed them as he knew he could return them to their sockets when he was at home.

He placed the skull inside the holdall, leaving the rest of the fox's remains to continue their journey back into the embrace of the earth the animal had once graced.

When he had the fox skull home he placed it on the kitchen table, and placed the small, sharp yellow teeth back in their sockets. The skull was more fragile than he had expected for a fox, almost cat-like and he placed it in a small clear glass case, positioned on the top shelf of the bookcase.

That night, when Sorley had again gone to bed alone, he was woken by the sound of Theresa entering the flat and the silence of her reaction when she went into the sitting room. In that silence he knew she had seen the skull and her finding it displaced the usual sounds of her return home – the kettle boiling, the night-time radio or TV news stations.

She came to the bedroom and turned on the main light.

'What is that, Sorley? In the sitting room.'

'The fox skull, I had to go back for it.'

'Why, Sorley? Why have you brought that thing back here? I can't and won't have it here,' she insisted.

Theresa then turned from the bedroom door and Sorley, realising her anger and her intentions, chased her until close to where the skull rested on its shelf. They struggled. Theresa was crying at the same time as he held her wrists tightly, close to his own chest.

'Get it out of here!' she yelled at him.

'No,' he said, 'it has to stay. It has to stay here with me.'

Theresa gave up her struggle and went back to the bedroom and Sorley slept on the sofa in the living room that night. He told himself it was because he felt the need to protect the skull, but he knew it was because they had argued and closeness seemed wrong. His sleep was shallow and tormented, sickened by the panicked rush of adrenaline that flowed through him after their struggle. They had never struggled like that before, but worse, he knew that he'd stood up to Theresa and the excuses she made for him. The questions were over and the doubts had all ended in that moment of struggle. He believed it all. None of it was insanity or the fall-out of his coma. The gift of sight, the flight, the cave, the saving of Calum, all of it was true, all of it was his and all of it related to another world, an archaic place and time where and when such things mattered. These were not gifts for the city, but gifts for the open wilderness.

When Sorley woke the flat was silent. He made tea and took it to Theresa in the bedroom. She was lying awake; her eyes were red with crying. She had one arm out of the bed, holding the covers close to her. Sorley could see skin burns on her wrists where he had held her during their struggle. She did not speak to him. He put the cup at her side and left the room. An hour later she came to the sitting room and they sat silently and awkwardly, waiting for some kind of reconciliation.

'Sorry,' said Sorley, 'I should have told you.'

'Why do we have to have it here, Sorley?'

'I want it here. I haven't been able to stop thinking about it.'

'Okay,' she said after a pause. 'Okay.'

'I want peace, Theresa. I need peace to recover. I need peace.'

'Yes,' replied Theresa, 'you will get it, I'm sure.'

Later, when Theresa was preoccupied and wouldn't notice what he was doing, Sorley stood in front of the bookcase and looked at the fox skull. He too was fearful of its hollow-eyed gaze that seemed to possess him whenever he stared into its blank orbits. But he could not now go back on his actions. It was too late.

The following morning Sorley went to the bookshop. The metal grille was down over the windows and the interior pitch black. He opened the door and was greeted by the dusty smell of old books and the faint note of dampness in the building. The wooden floor creaked as he walked to the back of the shop and turned on the main lights, two long neon tubes that hung on dust-covered chains from the ceiling. The glass doors on the cabinets behind the counter were closed but had been polished and the books behind that glass were clean and stood neatly on their ends. Everything was in order. The till was open and the cash inside was only that of the small float he kept in case he made a cash sale early in the day.

The books on top of the counter were new to the shop and Sorley knew then that Danny had been keeping the business going for him while he was away. He'd repay him for that. Sorley was glad to be back at his work and was glad that he came back to order rather than chaos.

Sorley placed the books he had carried with him almost constantly since the beating on the counter. The Rasmussen he'd file under anthropology. He dusted its cover. The pages were too crimped to enable sale at anything like a decent price or even prominence for the large book in the window. Who in the west end of the city would want knowledge of the 'intellectual culture of the Iglulik Eskimos' anyway? It was the kind of title he could sell on the net if only he had ever got round to getting a site sorted out. In its current condition the book was nearly worthless, but someone, just like he had, would buy it out of curiosity.

As he placed the title on the shelf among other books of a similarly obscure even arcane provenance it dawned on him to have a sale, to offer the static stock of the shop at sale prices. He'd change the window and put out the sandwich board with the word 'sale' written on it in chalks. He'd offer anthropology, comparative religion and even some titles from the philosophy and 'dark arts' shelves at a fraction of the cost written inside their front covers.

As he dusted and filed books, taking the odd title from the shelves here and there with the sale shelves in mind, the door opened.

'Hello?' queried the voice and Sorley knew at once that it was Danny and peered round the corner of the bookcase.

'Hello, Danny, *ciamar a tha thu?*' he asked him in the simple, jokey Gaelic that always began their conversation.

'*Tha mi alright, tapaidh leat, ciamar a tha thu fhèin?*'

'*Tha gu math,*' and they began laughing at that point, the same point they always gave up at in the mother tongue.

'How's it feel to be back?' Danny asked him.

'Good. Really great,' Sorley replied. 'Thanks for holding the fort, I owe you one.'

'It was nothing, quite enjoyed it, to tell you the truth, makes a change from the four walls on a rainy day. Grace will be asking after you.'

'Well, I'm fine now, you can tell her, just fine. You bought some new titles?' Sorley asked Danny.

'Aye, just the ones that looked in good condition, only a few pounds each, maybe something for you in one of them,' replied Danny.

'I'm thinking of having a sale, get rid of some of this old stock.'

'Right, freshen it up a little, I'll give you a hand if you like?'

'You getting into the book trade Danny?'

'No, just getting out of the house . . .'

'Let me buy you lunch, a trip to MacFarlane's for a pie.'

'Aye, all right,' replied Danny, 'but only one, mind.'

MacFarlane's lounge was a dark-wood and cut-glass relic, a cavernous Victorian establishment that was busy all day and all who ventured in mixed steadily, if not happily, in the lounge.

'A Jameson's and a half, please,' Sorley asked the barman, 'and a pint of Guinness,' he added. The barman acknowledged Sorley with faint recognition.

'Have you any pies left? Two if you've got them?'

'Aye, and how are you now? I was told you took a beating a while back,' said the barman unexpectedly, as he placed the three glasses on the counter in front of Sorley.

'Oh, fine now, thanks. I was a little shaken for a while there. A thing like that can really put you off your pint.'

'Aye, sure. Did they get anyone for it yet?'

'Not that I'm aware of. Nobody local seemed to know who he was and since I came out I haven't had a call from the police. I'm assuming now that it has all been filed away and forgotten.'

'Well, you should be careful. There are some rough cunts about the city these days, some real rough cunts. Did he take your wallet or anything?'

'No, just gave me a beating within an inch of my life. He really wanted to kick the shit right out of me.'

'Sure . . .' said the barman, nodding and turning to serve a woman who had entered the bar with a couple of her friends. Mascara was smudged around her eyes and ran in thick rivulets down her cheeks. Her hair was pulled from its normal grace and her pals seemed to want to fuss about her, getting her to a seat. But no, she was fine and would stay by the bar for a while.

'I'll bring the pies over.'

Sorley returned to the table in the corner where he sat with Danny and discussed the book sale. The pies came and after another round of drinks Danny said that he had to go.

Sorley remained behind. He'd take another drink and then go back to the shop and begin setting out the new display. He sat and watched as the women who had come into the bar just after he'd arrived continued to order vodka, but the one who seemed to need it most ordered rum and coke, which at first she sipped at and then downed rapidly as she recovered a little of her composure. The group of women went and sat at a table nearby and over an hour their number grew until there were maybe ten in a group around two tables. Sorley moved to the bar and continued drinking whisky and half-pints. By five o'clock he was pissed again.

After a while, the woman who had entered the bar crying, but who was now as relaxed as the others, left the group and came over to make an order. She carried with her a list of drinks written on a corner of newspaper and a roll of notes from a kitty kept in a glass. She gave the barman the paper list and he set about getting the drinks, placing them on a tray as he got them.

Sorley looked at the woman. She was, he thought, about twenty-five, or maybe twenty-eight. Attractive with dark hair and a small round face. He did not think twice about talking to her. He felt for some reason that he knew her well.

'Are you feeling okay now?' he asked her.

'Yes, fine now, thank you,' she replied with a little surprise and hesitation in her voice at the stranger's question.

'Good, you've got a few friends with you now anyway, that's always a comfort.'

'Yes . . .'

'Here, let me give you a hand with that . . .' said Sorley, getting off the bar-stool as he moved to help the woman whose name he did not know take the tray of drinks over to her friends.

'Thank you,' she said as he placed the tray down on one of the tables the party was occupying. She turned and went back to the bar to pay.

'Hello, I'm Sorley, by the way . . .'

'Oh, hi, hello . . . Kathleen.'

Then a difficult silence fell between them as the barman went to get her change from the roll of notes.

'So,' Sorley began again, 'just broken off with your man?'

'Something like that,' she said in a tone that acknowledged Sorley's obviously drunken forwardness.

'Sorry,' he said, 'that's none of my business. Sorry.'

'No,' she said, 'it's not.'

The barman returned with her change and she left carrying her own drink back to the group. Sorley ordered a double Jameson's and poured a little water into it.

'Women, eh?'

'For sure,' said the barman.

Sorley slowly forgot the awkwardness of the conversation with Kathleen. He was only trying to be friendly. Or maybe he was just lonely sitting there, drinking for the sake of drinking and thought nothing more of it.

Then the quiet calm of the lounge bar was shattered. The dark-wood and cut-glass swing doors that opened into that usually calm space suddenly broke open under the charge of a young man in an expensive dark suit jacket, who stood for a second looking around him and then made straight for Kathleen's table.

The women at that table let out a shriek and screamed as the young man approached. Kathleen turned on her seat. The women were up on their feet but they could not prevent the young man from grabbing hold of Kathleen's arm and pulling her until she fell from the stool and was on the ground at his feet.

The barman rushed from behind the bar and was yelling at the young man to leave the premises, pushing him as he spoke. But the young man would not let go of the woman on the floor and a tussle was developing with the barman and the other women. In the middle of it all, with drinks, chairs and the table falling around her, was Kathleen, who was now sobbing uncontrollably once again.

Sorley got off his bar-stool and made for the young man, shouting as he did so. The man did not respond and Sorley grabbed him by the neck and with his free arm drove the edge of a cut-glass ashtray onto the young man's nose. Blood jetted instantly from the site of the impact and the man rocked backwards with the force of the blow.

Bleeding heavily, he struggled to free himself from Sorley's grip.

The barman took the man's other arm and bent it sharply behind his back and the two of them led him to the door and flung him onto the street, warning him not to return.

When the fighting was over, Kathleen sat crying. Sorley's heart was pounding violently in his ribcage with the adrenaline rush of the attack. Others who had witnessed the incident worked to put right the chairs and tables that had been knocked over. The barman swept up broken shards of glass into a dustpan before fixing drinks for Kathleen, her party and Sorley.

Sorley had blood on his hands and shirt again. He buttoned his coat to cover the red stains and went to the dark-tiled bathroom to wash the stains off his hands.

'Thanks for that,' said the barman when Sorley returned to his stool. 'Can I get you anything?'

'Aye, I'll take another double, port and brandy if that's okay, settle the nerves.'

'Sure.'

Sorley went over to Kathleen. She was crying with her head in her hands. He placed an arm around her shoulder and tried to reassure her.

'It's okay, he's gone now and won't be back'. But Kathleen was beyond consoling just then and he left her with her friends.

Sorley sat drinking on his own again. A few of those who had witnessed the incident came over and offered him drink, condolences and congratulations in equal mixture on the force of his intervention. Sorley took the drinks.

Kathleen came to him at the bar.

'Thanks for your help,' she said, drying the corners of her eyes.

'Oh, it's nothing. It's okay, if you are?'

'Yes, I am now, thank you.'

'A bad sort to be mixing with – not me, I mean your friend,' said Sorley.

'Aye,' said Kathleen, 'always has been.'

'You've been with him long?'

'Too long, but that's it finished.'

'Isn't that what they all say, then tomorrow you'll return to him?'

'Not this time.'

'Can I get you a drink?' asked Sorley.

'Yes, thank you.'

Sorley motioned to the barman who served the wine from an already uncorked bottle. Kathleen sipped from the glass.

'I was in a fight myself a few weeks back,' he said.

'Oh?' said Kathleen.

'I've been in two fights since I left school and they've both been in the last six months. Crazy that, isn't it?'

'It must be in your stars.'

'It's in my waters, more like.'

As the conversation continued, broken and stilted as it was, Sorley began to feel more and more nauseous. He hadn't eaten since the pie at lunchtime and he had started to drink rum to try and quell the pain. His head was aching. He was sweating and his hands had started to tremble.

'Are you okay?' Kathleen had asked him.

'Aye, I will be soon, but I need some fresh air,' he said, rising from the bar-stool. Fearing that he was going to vomit, he left the bar and found a quiet place in the dark alleyway at the side of the bar. There, leaning against the damp brickwork, a shaking fit took hold of him.

'Christ,' he said to himself below his breath.

He was shivering and lay down on the ground beside the bar's rubbish bins. He found a bundle of woven plastic sacks, each of which was flecked with the remains of raw meat but he didn't care that their condition was less than hygienic; they would warm him, he thought, maybe help stop the shaking. He pulled the sacks over his quaking body, covering his head with them as though they were blankets and he lay with the faint smell of rancid meat fat surrounding his head and lapsed quickly into a cold, shivering, coma-like sleep.

In his fevered sleep, he was then taken from the dark alleyway, taken with the butcher's blankets on his back. He heard again the lapping of the waves and he was in the wooden, oar-less boat, drifting into the bay and to the now familiar shore. He did not fly this time but walked away from the dunes and out onto the high moorland.

He was walking beside a dry-stone wall that stretched many miles ahead of him over the moors, thick with purple heather and yellow mosses. On the wall, calling to him and seeming to lead him onwards, was a chorus of small birds.

He could feel the cold breeze of spring and faint warmth from the watery sun on his face. He started to run beside the wall as though he was a child elated upon experiencing wilderness for the first time. He ran panting heavily until he reached the summit of a low hill.

On the other side of the hill he saw the grey shallows of a loch stretching out before him. But here the sun had given way to mist, a mist that shrouded the land.

He could not see if there were tall hills beside the shores of the loch, or just more miles of indifferent moorland. He walked to the loch edge and there on the banks he found the carcass of a small deer.

On the other bank, barely visible but clearly crying, was Kathleen. She was beckoning him towards the deer. He stood above it. Blood did not run from the wounds of the deer but its flesh had bruised a deep magenta colour. The once red-brown skin on its hindquarters was turning crimson with the blood flow trapped inside below the surface. Blood was curdling in its muscles.

With a sharp stone from the loch edge, Sorley cut open the bruised flesh and saw beneath it the broken bones of the deer.

From the mist, face down in the loch water, the body of a young man – the man he had wrenched from Kathleen – then slowly drifted towards him. Then darkness came again.

Sorley slowly came round. The sack blankets had been pulled from his face and Kathleen stood weeping above him. The shivering and sweating of his drunken fit had left his body.

She helped him to his feet, relieved that he was able to walk. They returned to the bar and he ordered and downed a double dark rum. Kathleen drank wine.

She was drunk. He was drunk. She held the bar for stability. He sat unsteadily on a bar-stool.

'I want to help you,' Sorley said.

'You can't. What can you do?'

'I want to help . . . I don't know. I just want to help.'

'There is nothing you can do. It's too late, I have to sort this out myself.'

'But you can't. You'll go back to him.'

'I won't, it's finished.'

'Let me help.'

'You can't help me Sorley. I don't know you,' she added more insistently.

'You do know me. This is all there is to know.'

'I need to go,' said Kathleen nervously.

'No, listen. Give me your address. I want to help, Kathleen.'

'But you can't. No one can help me now.'

'Please, let me at least try.'

'No. I don't need your help.'

'Please, let me at least try,' said Sorley again, but this time he held her forearm.

Kathleen reluctantly gave him her address. He kissed her cheek as he left the bar.

Sorley returned home after midnight. He turned the key in the door of the flat and instead of the shouting he expected to be greeted with he found only darkness and silence. The flat was empty. Theresa had gone. But Sorley would not try to find her that night. He would leave her alone wherever she was. Leave her with her anger.

The following morning, hungover with the intake of the previous day, Sorley found the scrap of paper in his coat pocket. He held it tight in his fist, shaken by memories of the struggle and fear that he had forced himself on the woman at the bar, but then he thought this would be his chance, he knew it was ridiculous but at least it might give him some outlet for his gifts.

He looked up at the fox skull and saw its face as it had been, the dry flesh of its lip on its newly exhumed remains. He saw again the bruised flesh of the deer by the lochside and felt its skin tugging and snagging as he cut through to the bones with a small sharp stone. He was back beside the railway track in the fading evening light, spade in hand, dragging the body of the fox towards the hole. He knew, as memories of the previous evening returned to him, he would help Kathleen.

In the late afternoon, still hungover, he left the flat and drove from the city out towards the highland lochs, not knowing what he was searching for. Way beyond the boundaries of the city, in the gathering dark of the late afternoon, he stopped the car beyond a sharp bend in the road where the loch shallows were closest to the low stone wall.

Torch in hand, he walked into the cover of a dense clump of stunted silver birches that came down a steep slope to meet the road. The faint blue haze of an icy mist was gathering between the trees. He would search the forests, the overgrown verges, the gullies and embankments of that stretch of road. It was notorious as a place where deer gathered after dark and was the scene of many a car accident and it was not long before he found the remains of a deer, road-kill fallen just yards from the site of a collision.

From its condition Sorley could tell that the deer must have been hit at speed on the road but had survived for a brief while and was able to walk for long enough to haul itself into the cover of the trees. There it had fallen down and died from its wounds leaving no trace on the road of that incident but a few fragments of coloured glass.

Sorley pulled the long blade of his Swiss Army knife from its red block and cut into the hard flesh of the beast where it appeared to be most bruised. The flesh ripped under the knife and beneath the skin shattered bones protruded through the crimson muscle flesh of the deer's hindquarters.

He picked a broken segment, pungent with marrow, from the wound, put it inside the holdall, and returned to the car. He had, he realised as he drove back to the city with the Radio 3 evening concert filling his car with Viennese waltz music, grown blasé towards these acts of animal butchery.

When he returned to the flat, there was still no sign of Theresa. He took the holdall into the kitchen and did not bother to inspect or clean the deer bone any further. He placed the bones in a large padded envelope and wrote a note to Kathleen on the back of the scrap of paper that she had written her address on for him.

The note read simply: 'Leave these with him'. Sorley did not include any note of his own address or reference to their conversation in MacFarlane's. Before sealing the envelope he took the fox skull from its position on top of the bookcase and rested it for a few moments on the bubble-wrap that now held the deer bones and then sealed the envelope.

It was then, as he was writing Kathleen's address on the envelope, that he heard a key turn in the front-door lock. Theresa had returned. When she entered the flat she did not, as he had thought she would, come into the kitchen to greet him with a row. Instead she went into the sitting room and sat quietly on her own.

When he had finished labelling the envelope, he took the fox skull back into the sitting room and placed it back on the shelf above where Theresa was sitting.

'Sorry,' he said, 'I should have called you.'

'Why?' asked Theresa. 'What good would that have done?'

'I thought you might have been worried about me?'

'No. You hoped I would be worried about you.'

'Sorry, I'm sorry. I can't turn the clock back now.'

'No, you can't. What are you doing with that thing out again?' Theresa asked, gesturing towards the fox skull.

'Nothing . . . I was just using it, that's all.'

'Using it? What do you mean using it?'

'There was trouble in MacFarlane's, a fight.'

'You weren't hit again?'

'No. This time I was doing the hitting.'

'What is going on? I can't leave the house without something happening to you. This can't go on, every time I turn my back on you something happens.'

'It was nothing. Just a man attacking a woman, and I pulled him away. There was a bit of a scuffle. That was all.'

'What's that skull got to do with that then?'

'I offered to help her out afterwards.'

'What do you mean, help her out?'

'I said I'd help her get rid of him.'

'And how are you going to do that, with voodoo I suppose?'

'Kind of . . .'

'What? What have you said to this woman?'

'Nothing, only I said I'd help her get away from him.'

'Well, is she here then?'

'No. I'm posting it to her.'

'What are you posting to her?'

'Some deer bone I found out by the loch.'

'Deer bone, dear God, more like . . . what have you promised this woman?'

'I said I'd help her out.'

'I give up, Sorley, I really do give up. I don't see you all day, you stay out and when I return I find you packing bones up in a parcel to send to a woman I've never met and who you've been fighting over in a bar. Does that not sound like insanity to you?'

'Sorry,' he said again, knowing how pathetic his apologies sounded.

Theresa was silent for a moment, and then she walked from the room towards their bedroom. Sorley didn't follow her this time. Theresa did not leave the bedroom that night.

The following morning, Theresa was up when Sorley woke. He dressed and found Theresa sitting at the kitchen table, holding the package addressed to Kathleen.

Sorley took it from her, put on his coat and went to the post office and posted the package to Kathleen.

A week after the incident at MacFarlane's, Sorley and Theresa made love for the first time since he had left hospital. It was at the end of one of her occasional days off and they had spent the entire day together in the flat.

They had not that day discussed anything to do with Sorley's troubles or the fight in MacFarlane's. Perhaps Theresa too was making an effort to try to normalise their daily lives, as much as was possible at that time.

But Sorley knew that she was harbouring a fear for the future, for their future together. She was uneasy, almost offensive with politeness in a way that Sorley understood to be a sign of her distance from him and the damage that the last few weeks and months had done to their relationship.

The morning after they made love, Sorley was in bed. Theresa had left the bedroom to make tea. It was an opportunity for them to relax in the morning, a time of the day when they normally rarely saw each other.

Sorley turned on the radio. The BBC Scotland news broadcast reported that the bodies of a young man and woman had been found dead in a car, half-submerged in Loch Lomond, close to a notorious danger spot. They had both drowned, or died of their injuries, after their car broke through the low wall at the side of the loch.

They had both sustained multiple injuries in the crash. The man's name was not being released until the next of kin had been informed. Strathclyde Police named the female occupant of the car as Kathleen Hughes, a twenty-eight-year-old woman from the west end of Glasgow.

Sorley turned off the radio. Theresa was standing in the bedroom doorway holding two mugs of tea. She looked at him in silence. He looked away from her gaze, unable to bear the force of horror in her eyes.

'Is that her, Sorley, the one you helped?'

'Yes, I think so. It's the same name.'

Theresa placed the mugs on the dressing table, sat in the only chair in their bedroom, and cried, both of her hands covering her face. Sorley did not try to comfort her.

He could not piece together how it all could have gone so badly wrong, unless she had wanted it to, unless she had taken her own life. She had gone back to him, that much he knew. Perhaps she had secreted the deer bone in the car without her boyfriend knowing but then he would not go on that journey without her and he had forced her to go with him, maybe violence had again been involved. He had won. That young, stupid man had triumphed; Kathleen had never managed to get the better of him, never managed to free herself of him. But why should he care? Why should he give a damn about the stranger in the bar? The answer was simple: because he cared for himself. He wanted it to work.

Sorley left the bedroom and Theresa sitting there. He went to the sitting room and poured himself a large whisky. He downed it in one, and then poured a second full glass. He knew of no other way of facing the blackest day they had had since he was beaten up. It was, he thought, worse than the beating.

Later that day Sorley drove to the loch where the car and the two bodies had been found. The car was gone, and beside the low wall at the loch edge were the shattered remains of car lights. A police roadside board asked for any witnesses to the accident to come forward.

Sorley walked to the loch edge where Kathleen had died, and where her body must have remained for the hours of darkness after the accident. Beneath a sigh of cloud that traced a ghostly pattern across the sky above the loch that dawn, strapped in a car with the man she hated, she sat and died. Sorley saw the blood running from her head wound and he saw how her hands were reddened with blood.

He sat on the loch wall and for the first time since the beating he broke down in tears, thick heavy tears that fell like storm rain from his eyes. Why was he crying, he asked himself again, why should he care? Why was he so affected by the death of the young woman? He was crying, he knew, because he was helpless, useless, possessed by nothing more than a delusion of memories and self-anointed powers, too archaic to be of use in the world to which he had been returned and he was too crude a novice to make any use of the gifts he had acquired.

Sorley returned home and poured himself a large dram and sat desolately before the television. He flicked listlessly between the channels, watching the rolling news and sport channels before the late-night Gaelic programmes came on, a nature programme flying the coastline of the islands shot as though from the eye of a gull. The camera travelled slowly up the white sands and dunes of the island shoreline. It was his island. It was the island he was born on, the island in the west where he was raised, and which he had left as a young man. Sorley sat watching, transfixed by the beauty of the island as though seeing it for the first time.

He saw the clear waters that filled the shallow rock pools and the dark green seaweed floating in clear seawater. The presenter spoke in Gaelic above the pictures, spoke of Norse men and their conversion to Christianity that led to the island's shoreline being dotted with small ancient temples and each one dedicated to a saint. Archive footage replaced the flying camera, footage of men and women – a family, perhaps – out on the moors cutting peats, drinking tea by a large bell tent, smiling for the camera.

Sorley was then a child again walking across the moorland with his father, walking towards the peat banks they cut every year. His father was carrying a spade to cut the *ceap*, and Sorley would lift the *ceap* his father cut and would lay it in the wet, black earth of the *broinn*. His father would be measuring and cutting the width and breadth of peat they'd be cutting that year from each of the banks, and then slowly cutting down into the turf, scoring the surface ready for lifting. Sorley could hear his father saying the words: *'rùisg'*, *'riachadh'*, *'carcair'*.

Then he heard his father's angered voice calling to him to lay the thick cut turf neatly side by side so that it was sure and level under foot, and calling to him if he placed it too close to the peat bank to allow the cutting of the peat to be done with ease.

As the turf came away, so the peat was exposed, brown as though it was the skinned flesh of the moor, waiting to be cut again.

One day his father would walk the moor to the peats and carry with him just the spade, then when the turfing was done on maybe four or six banks, he would lift the *tairsgeir* from the butt in which it had been soaking for half a week to tighten the handle.

'Look, Sorley,' he would say, holding up the club-footed turf iron to the young boy, the same every year with the same incantation of the old names. '*Cas*, the handle; *smeachan*, the step; *na h-ailean*, the handle socket; *cro*, the heel; *sgian*, the knife; *faobhar*, the blade edge; *bàrr na sgeine*, the top of the blade . . . Cutting and throwing peat: the trick is never to get ahead of yourself. *Bàrr-fàd* – the first layer, above the bank. *Corrad* – the first peat, close out in front of you. The second peat in goes to the back leaving space for the rest, its edge turned towards you. The others go in between. Then move on as I cut until that layer is cut and we start the one beneath. *Fàd a' ghàrraid* – the peats of the wall. The second layer builds a small wall on the edge above the bank.'

And as he stood there, high on the *bàrr-fàd*, treading the *tairsgeir* slowly in and down, its depth and its width into the peat, his father would worry at the *snaidheadh*, the finish, or the dressing, of the inside wall of the bank ensuring that it was clean and smooth. And then he would be eye-to-eye with Sorley as they reached the *fàd a' caoran*, the bottom layer, above the hard broken cobbles of the base rock.

The *mòine dhubh*, the black peat, would rise wet and heavy from the *fàd a' caoran*, like a lamb being pulled from its mother. That peat was pungent with the sulphurousness of rotten plant matter, a smell they loved for it promised a hot, quick-lighting fire in the winter stove. They would wrench it from the rock beneath with a loud shlock, and with a rasp and grate from the *sgian* scratching on the hard.

The father spoke as they worked on:

'*Mòine dhubh*, black peat from the *fàd a caoran*. *Mòine bhan*, white peat rich in fibre that would keep a fire in all night.

'*Mòine chruaidh ghlas*, a mix of black and fibre peat that won't crumble like the *mòine dubh*.

'*Làrach isein*, leave a space at the edge of the bank.'

When all the peats had been cut and had been laid out on the moor drying for maybe two weeks, they would go out again to lift and turn them and dry them further, keeping the wet face to the sun.

Sorley and his father bent over the peats, lifting three into a *rudhan beag*, the small, almost dolmen-type structure made by leaning two against each other, wet side to the sun, with a small peat on top as a kind of flat crown.

When all had been lifted, they would return again and turn the peats in the *rudhan beag*, placing them to form a *rudhan*, the larger stack, and ready for taking home.

The day would arrive when the peats were dry and stacked ready for the tractor to carry them home across the moor. The tractor would tip them close to last year's stack, where they would lie until the mother built the *cruach*, the peat stack, building it with the diamond-shaped peats forming a herringbone wall.

And then day by day peat was taken in and children would play in the shelter of the *beul na cruaich*, the open end of the stack.

Each night Sorley's mother would take a wet peat from a pail she kept for the purpose and place it in the fire, keeping it alight over night. The night fire – *fàd tasgaidh a teine*.

As he sat in the room with the Gaelic programme flickering on the screen, Sorley heard his mother shouting at him the first night he came home drunk, calling him *proghan*, the soaked peat that keeps the fire in: the drunk man that stays up all night.

The programme finished and Sorley turned off the television set. He sat quietly in the room, thinking of his home island. He would go back. He would escape the last few months and return to the island. He would go alone. He could, so he would, escape.

Sorley thought of the small croft house his parents had left him and which he had left empty for years. It was, he thought, by now proba-bly half-derelict and uninhabitable. But the land surrounding it – the moors and dunes and the rolling hills that stretched into the middle of the island – these would remain, as they were when he was a child. These would be as they were when, day after day as a child enjoying the school break in the summer, he walked for miles without thinking that he was anything other than safe.

He thought of the steep cliff that fell away at the end of the croft, down towards the shore and the rocks there, which shattered the incom-ing waves to shards of white water. He had never felt any yearning for this place until now. He had never thought of it with reverence before.

When his parents had died he thought that they had left him only this small house and a few thousand pounds in a will that he had refused to take but which finally was sent to him by a solicitor. And now he saw that they had left him an ocean of peace, a place where life could begin again and where there was escape from the insanity of the city. Maybe it was a place where he would be wanted and he would be taking the gift home.

Sorley waited up for Theresa to come home. No sooner was she in the door in her uniform, smelling of hospitals, than he told her he needed to talk to her.

'Can't it wait?' she had asked him.

'No. No, I need to talk now.'

'Have you been drinking, Sorley?'

'No, that has nothing to do with it either.'

'Well, what is it then? I'm tired and can't stay up playing these daft word games with you?'

'I need to go away.'

'Well, speak to me tomorrow about it.'

'I can't, you're not here tomorrow.'

'So? So you want to go away. Well, go then,' she snapped, turning out of the room and heading to their bedroom.

Sorley did not go after her and he heard the bedroom door close.

The following morning Theresa woke Sorley. He had slept all that night in the living room in his best suit. She had made coffee for them both and came and sat on the edge of the sofa next to where he had been sleeping.

'Sorley, I want you to see somebody, talk over all that has happened.'

Sorley looked at Theresa in silence. He knew he had been drinking heavily and he felt some shame for the suddenness of his outburst the previous night.

'No, I won't,' he said. 'I don't think it would do any of us any good.'

'Fine. Well, go then,' said Theresa. 'I'm sick of you being drunk and fighting and wandering around in a dream world. Go. Go and run away home if you want to.'

'I will. I will go because I'm sick and tired of it all, too,' snapped Sorley in return.

'Your problem is that you can't see when you're not well. And you're not well now. All this rubbish you speak about visions and animal bones. You need to talk to someone about the trauma of the fight, not about bloody witchcraft.'

'It may be rubbish to you,' said Sorley, 'but to me it feels real, more real than the fight. That was surreal. It was strange, almost as though it didn't happen to me. I will be fine. I will. I just want time to work out what is going on.'

Theresa looked at him without answering. He looked away, unable to engage with the worry in her eyes. He walked to the window. Theresa's eyes followed him.

'Don't stare at me,' he said sharply.

She did not answer.

The following day Sorley searched through a box of letters and papers he kept – most were sentimental objects others were insurance policies, documents of some merit. In the pile he found what he was looking for, a card from their neighbour on the island. The man, who had known Sorley all his life from his childhood to the death of his parents, had asked Sorley to send him a key to the house so that he could keep an eye on it, keep it ventilated while Sorley was away. The card was browning with age now but Sorley had sent the key on as soon as it had arrived.

On the card was a telephone number.

Sorley dialled the number.

'Hello,' came the familiar voice.

'Hello, is that Alex?'

'It is, who's speaking please?'

'It's Sorley, Alex, Sorley from next door.'

'Sorley, how are you? It's lovely to hear your voice.'

'Alex, I'm fine, fine, it's just that I'm coming home, coming home for a while and I wondered . . .'

Alex interrupted him, '. . . if I could set the house right for you, of course, son, of course. We've kept an eye on it but, you know, they don't stay in good shape when they're not lived in for a long time. When are you coming?'

'In a day or so, soon anyway. I've no car so can't bring much with me this time, but if you could check the stove and lights and let me know if anything needs doing before I can come – better still if anything needs a fix urgently, I'll send on the money to you.'

'No, everything will be fine. I'll make sure of that. And will you be bringing your wife?'

'No, Alex, not this time, just coming alone for a break.'

'Very good, Sorley, very good, we'll be looking forward to seeing you now.'

'Aye, I'm looking forward to coming, it's been too long.'

'Well, that's very good, very good indeed.'

When Sorley heard Alex's voice he knew at once that he was making the right decision, almost as if the sound of a voice, the inflection of the Gaelic in the English, the shaping of vowels somehow changed the constitution of his blood. More of a transfusion than a journey, Sorley knew, or at least hoped he knew that going home would bring sense to the happenings of the last few weeks and months.

Sorley went to the bookshop. His journey took him past MacFarlane's but he avoided going in. The shop was in darkness. He opened the door, flicked on the dim light and stood looking about the forlorn, run-down interior. The front edges of the shelves were rounded with wear, the grain of their wood white with the polish of movement – books in and out, hands touching, pulling, half in, half out. The centres of the aisles were white, too, white with the passage of feet passing over the years.

He walked from case to case. In some places the shelves were more empty than usual, a sign of his neglect. Other shelves bulged with titles, a sign perhaps of his incompetence as a book buyer, too often buying what he found interesting rather than what had an obvious market.

Behind the counter were the dark-oak glazed bookcases that held the valuable titles, or the delicate titles, too fragile to have on the open shelves. The case was all but empty. The Gaelic titles had gone, the rare and the old, he often sold to libraries or collections. He'd a good eye for the old Gaelic and often he relied on those sales to keep the entire enterprise on its feet.

But now, he thought, it would all have to go. He was leaving, going home and for the first time acknowledged to himself that perhaps he was not coming back.

He picked up the receiver of the phone at the back of the shop and dialled Danny.

'Danny,' he began when the call was answered.

'Yeah, Sorley, what's fresh?' Danny replied.

'I'm thinking of going away for a while.'

'Going? Where are you going?'

'I'm going home, I need a break from all this stuff, the last few months have been difficult.'

'Yes, I know but is going away going to help that?'

'I think so, I think it's right, and, besides, what is there to stay for?

Theresa's not talking now, she wants space and I haven't been well.'

'You've troubles, Sorley, I know that, but sometimes it's best to stay and deal with things head on.'

'These troubles are more difficult than that – these troubles take you away from people. People think you're mad with these troubles.'

'There's no trouble you can't talk to me and Grace about, we're here for you, anytime.'

'Thank you for that, I know, and it's a comfort to me. But look, I'll need to do something with the shop. I don't want to sell until I know what I'm doing.'

'You want me to take it on for a while?'

'Aye, till I'm back in form and favour.'

'That's no bother at all. I said I'd help you if I could, and I will. I think I told you, I'm away for a little while myself, go to the hills for a time.'

'That's no bother, any help to keep it going would be good just now.'

'Okay, leave it to me and keep in touch.'

'Yes, thanks, Danny.'

He hung up and sat in the old chair behind the counter. He looked about the interior once again. He was leaving it all behind. Heavy tears began to roll from his eyes, and as they fell scenes from the last few months filled his mind. The beating, the cave, the stones, the body, the fox, flying, flying, flying north, the beauty of snow blue with moonlight on a dark night. The beauty of the waves curling across the sands of a bay. The calling of birds: gulls, crows and eagles. The howling of fox and wolf; *mallachadh, marbh-phaisg, taghairm*. The gift of sight, the gift of healing, the gifts of the Earth of love and loss and abundance.

Sorley's tears were those of joy. If recent events had cast off the ties and bonds of his previous life, so however marked with sadness, he had been freed and now he would be free to follow the gift.

The books he had prepared for the sale were stacked in a pile beside the last bookcase before the counter. At the base was the beaten copy of Rasmussen's work. He'd take it as a memento, he thought. It had become like an old friend, seen him when he was half-dead; seen him as he really was. Maybe he'd even get the time to read it back on the island.

FOUR

The ferry backed from the quayside and turned to face its prow into the waves and the long, narrow line of the steep-sided sea loch that led to open waters.

Sorley stood on the top deck of the boat. The wind was fierce and sharp with cold and numbed his face as the boat slowly pulled out into the sea.

Few of the other passengers on board stood with him on the open deck, most had made for the bar or restaurant, and would not venture outside unless they became desperate for a smoke.

Of the few who stood watching on the outer decks, watching as the boat slowly drew away from the mainland, a young couple, tourists he assumed, admired the view while hugging and kissing.

The mountains behind the small village port were still capped with snow, the jagged white line of their summits cutting into the pale blue sky. Beneath the row of high summits, a brown and purple plain stretched down into the dark blue waters of the loch.

Away from the village port, large, isolated houses hugged the loch shore at the bottom of seemingly impossible roads. Soon, even the sparse density of these few outlying houses had shrunk to zero and the boat glided through a landscape freed of people with no trees, just moorland broken by the deep gouging of water on its passage to the sea.

It was a land he knew well from the numerous journeys he had made from the island to the mainland and the mainland to island, and was smoothed by a low forest of heather and bracken and broken by steep-sided cliffs that towered above the waterline. The boat sailed past and the gradual undulation of the land pointed to the closeness of the open sea.

Looking north, Sorley could see the first lights of hamlets up the coast coming into view, small coastal villages ringed by white sand, home to remote communities founded on the sea and crofting but now declined; home to those who loved the isolation and wild beauty of the landscape, the raging seas of winter and the pure, intoxicating air that in summer was pungent with the aromatics of the highland forest and the sea.

To the south, peering silently over the low brow of the fjord's forming hills, a larger mountain stretched its limbs in three of the four directions of the compass. Its summit held back darker clouds that threw their shadows onto the ridges and into the corries that formed the uppermost slopes of the mountain. Its arms reached towards him, as though offering an embrace.

Slowly the almost enclosed waters of the loch gave way to open sea, but the calm loch did not resign itself to the might of the ocean with ease but fought over a mass of half-hidden rocks and razor-edged skerries. The loch mouth was scattered with these small islands, cluttering and confusing the waves and forming narrow, open channels for the boat to sail through. Sometimes the land of these islands seemed to the traveller so close that he could almost touch it as the ferry passed by.

Sorley read the names of these islands on a board by the door to the open passenger deck, but in truth he did not need the words on that board; he knew them all, each one, and each had in turn played host to some childhood fantasy of survival and shipwreck:

Isle Martin
Iolla Mhor
Horse Island
Sgeir Revan
Na Finlaichean
Eilean Dubh
Stac Mhic Aonghais
Glas Leac Beag
Isle Ristol
Glas Leac Mor
Eilean Mullagrach
Tanera Mor
Tanera Beag

. . . and out in the sea as though discarded by the land, the jagged rock of *Eilean a Char*.

Sorley said the names again and again in his head. As their sounds resonated so the sun broke over the exposed, ice-scoured rock of a sea cliff, its reflection a brilliant orange in the deep blue waters of the loch.

The boat made its way through these narrow channels and out beyond, out into the open waters. At its side, shearwaters and gannets skimmed the waves, finding hidden ways between the rolling tide, the surf and ripple of white breaking water. The wind rattled salted flag ropes, the colour of weathered bones on their hollow poles, a chinking, clinking patter and the ferry's engines roared through their red funnels pushing the boat on in defiance of the growing swell.

Out on the ocean, Sorley saw white water break and waves rolling in steady rhythm. In the lee of the waves isolated birds floated, dived, surfaced, the epitome of loneliness – always the shearwaters, the auk, the little auk, the smallest of the birds in the ocean – it's always the smallest that is alone and, he wondered, does the bird live in awe of the waves, the sea, the sky that rings its being? Was he not the bird in those waves, migrating, running like a salmon back to its first home, the gravel bed, the river source – running, flying, diving, awash in isolation?

What else is there, he thought, but awe for the waves, awe for the sky, awe for the mountains and all that remains is the Earth and its love is the strongest, the loneliest of all.

The ferry docked at the terminal in Stornoway. The quayside was bustling with folk, some coming, some going, others meeting loved ones with tearful hugs and kisses and a slow walk with a heavy bag or a heavy heart back to a car waiting in the car park.

Sorley joined the short queue for a cab and when his turn came he gave the address to the driver who did not know the house. He had not, he said, ever taken a fare there in all his years of driving a taxi.

'No, probably not, it's been empty for some while now,' replied Sorley to the driver's enquiries.

When he arrived at the cottage darkness had fallen and the only features Sorley could make out of the surrounding landscape were the steep drop to the beach that sank away from the end of the croft some two hundred yards from the house and, on the other side of the cottage, the crofts that led out to the dunes and a cluster of small croft houses grouped before the shore.

The door of the cottage was unlocked. The interior was warm but with the background dankness that damp brings to a house when it has lain empty. The sound of the waves breaking on the shore was clearly audible from inside the house and it was a sound he knew from his childhood; then, it was subsumed by familiarity to the status of the inaudible, now after years of absence, it was as loud as a howling gale.

Sorley flicked on the light switch in the narrow hall at the front of the house but the lights remained off and he struck a match and fumbled his way forward in the darkness to the kitchen.

By the stove he found a small basket of peats, coal and wood beside the stove in the kitchen, and on the table a note in fine handwriting: 'Sorley, welcome home. The house electric has not been reconnected yet, maybe Monday or Tuesday, but there are candles and matches and fuel, some milk in the pantry. Cook in the stove until the place is hooked up again! Alex.'

Sorley carried his bag from the front door and left it in the middle of the kitchen floor, opened the blue enamel doors of the old Rayburn stove and began making the fire.

With the stove lit, he sat in the large, deep armchair that was wedged between the cold side of the stove and a small window that looked out towards the machair and the houses by the beach. It was the chair in which his father had sat winter through winter, his slippers off, his feet in their thick woollen socks balanced on the edge of the hot-plate warming but not burning, the dog curled under his legs, its nose resting on the floor.

Sorley pushed the small window open. The night air was full of the sound of the breaking waves and sheep out on the grazings calling through the veil of drizzle that fell. He could see the faint lights of trawlers miles out in the Minch, returning to harbour.

He fumbled through his bag and found the battery-powered radio he always carried. He lit another two candles and settled in the immediate comfort of the kitchen without bothering to look through the rest of the cottage. He tuned the radio to the Gaelic station, sat in the chair as the heat of the stove began to be felt in the air of the room, pulled the thick leather of his coat up around his body, and slowly fell asleep.

*   *   *

Sorley woke the following morning with the radio still playing. The candles had burned down to two dark rings in their soot-stained saucers and bright blue morning light was streaming through the small window by the armchair in which he had spent the night asleep.

He looked from the kitchen window towards the calm, deep blue waters of the Minch and the white, rugged outlines of the far Sutherland Hills heading north on their journey along the mainland coast until they died in a slump of shallow angles and turned the corner of Cape Wrath.

The air was cooled by a north wind, layered with sea salt, peat smoke and the smell of sheep. The machair was cut with the spikes of lemon-green marram grass and was deep with almost pure white sand.

A dog barked from somewhere near the shore houses. Sheep bleated. But nobody was to be seen. The single-track road that passed close by the cottage and led onto the vast open beaches of the north was silent and empty. Nobody had driven that way that morning.

Sorley unpacked his bag in the kitchen. He took a bundle of clothes out and placed them on the small wooden table. He unfolded the flat layers of shirts, jeans and thick jumpers and pulled the fox skull from a protected enclave he had made for it in the heart of the bundle.

He placed the skull centre stage on the bare wooden shelf above the stove. Beside it he put the two white saucer candlesticks. The chosen place was right for the skull. Its white grimace and hollow eyes surveyed the room. No longer just the simple domestic room of a cottage but the centre of a discreet shrine. It would remind him of why he came back.

He sat in the armchair listening to the singers on the Gaelic station. As he listened he looked through the small kitchen window, out towards the machair. Although still morning-time the year had advanced such that the daylight was fading and seemed to fail from dawn to dusk until it finally gave way to the weight of darkness massed against it to the east.

The sky that day had turned from light blue and white to peach and light purple with massive swollen bales of pale orange cumulus clouds drifting above the Minch, heading north on the almost constant south-westerlies that blew to the east side of the island from the wild Atlantic coast.

As he looked out over the coast and the distant mountains of Sutherland, a voice came from the radio, sorrowful and keening, seeming ancient in its tone and melody, a voice that, could they sing, could have been that of the moorland or the machair.

Ochòin a laoigh, leag iad thu,
Leag iad thu, laoigh, leag iad thu
Ochòin a laoigh, leag iad thu,
'M bealach a' ghàrraidh

'S truagh nach robh mis 'an sin
'S ceathr' air gach làimh dhomh

Ochòin a laoigh, leag iad thu,
Leag iad thu, laoigh, leag iad thu
Ochòin a laoigh, leag iad thu,
'M bealach a' ghàrraidh

An leann thog iad gu d'bhanais
Air d'fhalairidh bha e

Ochòin a laoigh, leag iad thu,
Leag iad thu, laoigh, leag iad thu
Ochòin a laoigh, leag iad thu,
'M bealach a' ghàrraidh

Bha mi'm bhréidich am ghruagaich
'S am bhanntraich 's an aon uair ud

Ochòin a laoigh, leag iad thu,
Leag iad thu, laoigh, leag iad thu
Ochòin a laoigh, leag iad thu,
'M bealach a' ghàrraidh

Gun chron air an t-saoghal ort
Ach nach d'fheud thu saoghal buan fhàistinn

Ochòin a laoigh, leag iad thu,
Leag iad thu, laoigh, leag iad thu
Ochòin a laoigh, leag iad thu,
'M bealach a' ghàrraidh

The sky darkened as he listened. A storm was approaching and the lighthouse on the far peninsula shone as brightly as though seen at night, its light turning to him and lighting the far wall of the kitchen before turning its beam away.

In the blackout the lighthouse was only visible as a narrow needle of white jutting from the headland and the kitchen was momentarily cloaked in its darkness.

Sorley watched the light turn again and again. The radio continued its songs; some he knew from when he was young and others were new to him but all were fierce in their poignant beauty; the shapes of the melodies undulating as softly as the dunes, and all fused in a moment of connection between the song, the light and the landscape.

A piper played the opening phrases of a pibroch, its rhythm slowly fading into that of the lighthouse. A woman's voice came in above the pipes. Sorley MacRath with the singer, the piper, the lighthouse and the landscape were all borne on the beam of light and the cry of the pipes. He was flying again and in the song he heard, as though coming from the distance, the slow beat of the shaman's drum. Its skin was from the north, its voice from the north and in the ancient voice was the voice of the Norse, the Inuit, the Sami and the Gael, all as one in one moment, all following the same drum. In its ancient skin of the drum was the spirit of the animal, the spirit of the person, the shaman dancing with them both on the skin of the drum. The rhythm a path to ecstasy, they danced on and on.

The light turned, the singer sang the song, the Gaelic song not far from the shaman, close, close as souls in the cave, close as Shony and Sedna, and Sorley was then high above the cottage, his arms outstretched. Shrouded in the black blanket of his wings he was invisible against the sky to all those rooted to the earth. His ears filled once more with the sound of gently lapping waves and the open thwarts of the boat were cold against his naked arms.

The boat drifted silently into the bay. He walked to the shore through the shallow waves that broke about his bare feet. The bone arches stood out in the darkness. He walked far inland. With the stride of a giant he traversed countless miles of moorland and then into the forest. The massing of conifers half-buried in deep snow did not slow him. He walked on, sometimes thigh deep in the snow and then stopped. His walking had been effortless as though he was above the land, walking beneath the star blanket.

Sorley remained still and in silence; his heart was pounding, not from the exertion of walking but from the force of exhilaration that rushed through his veins. He was in awe at the majesty of the land, the vast openness of the star-filled sky and he was silenced by the vast landscape.

He walked on to the banks of a river and saw the red moon reflected in the flow of water. The red moon was the blood of winter warming in the river's flow, dissolving its red clot where clear, white tree-blood, spilt and clotted in an autumn storm drifted in corms over rock silts, grey in the shallows of the river's crura.

Sorley knelt in the river. Cold blue river-blood flowed through his fingers and he clawed at the riverbed for what was buried there. He clawed until he was gasping for air and then he lay exhausted in the river and its waters forked around his body.

He was a new island and tree-blood could spawn on his banks. His skin would be the land of the island until a winter storm would bring waters burdened with force-split timbers and rounded stones down upon him, and he'd shed the land skin and lie on dry ground, vulnerable to the hooded crows until new flesh grew about him.

He walked back towards the shore and the boat. The pipes and drum were closer now and he rose again into the darkness, away from the lapping waves and the bone arches.

He was back in the kitchen. The lighthouse shone its bright beam towards him, filling the room with light. The radio played a final pibroch, the notes of which were placed in the air like the ground stones of a dyke dug deep into the land.

The following day Sorley was sleeping in the armchair in the kitchen after walking the moors. A knock on the door followed by the sound of the handle turning woke him with a start. A face, that of an older man, was looking into the half-darkness of the room and from behind the man an aged black-and-white collie walked into the room.

'*A bheil duine an seo?*' asked the visitor.

'*Aye, fàilte, thig a-staigh!*' said Sorley, getting up from the chair.

'Alex,' he said, when he realised who it was.

'Sorley,' replied Alex, holding out a hand. Sorley took the hand and instead of a simple polite shake Alex held on to the hand in a warm embrace.

'Welcome home, son, it's good to see life about the house again. How are you settling back?'

'Grand, Alex, just grand, and thanks for the fire and milk and getting the place open again.'

Alex finally let go Sorley's hand.

'No bother at all, Sorley. No bother.'

'Can I get you anything?' asked Sorley. 'Will you take a seat for a while, take a dram, perhaps?' he said, with a glint of recognition in his eye.

'Ha, go on, one won't do me any harm.'

Alex sat at the table while Sorley rooted in the bag for the half bottle he'd bought before getting the ferry.

Alex barked a command quietly to the dog: '*laigh sios*', and the dog lay down by the stove without further command from Alex, resting its head on its outstretched front paws.

'*Slàinte mhath*,' said Alex, raising his glass.

'*Slàinte*,' repeated Sorley as they both drank from their glasses.

'The place will be awfully cold for a while until you can get it aired,' said Alex.

'Aye, it's frightening how quickly a place like this shows signs of falling in. I left it too long,' replied Sorley.

'Yes, it goes like that. It's easy to leave, but nigh-on impossible to get back once you've gone,' said Alex and they sat for a few seconds in an awkward silence.

'It was a tragedy, the way your mother and father went, so sudden and close by one another,' began Alex.

'Aye,' said Sorley as though acknowledging that the easiest discussion for them was about the old times.

'You have a family now yourself, Sorley?'

'No . . . I mean, yes, of sorts . . . a wife in Glasgow, but no children.'

'She's not coming back with you?'

'Not this time. She's working in the hospital, difficult to get away and I needed to look over this place for a while,' replied Sorley, not sure if he was a convincing liar or not.

'It's sad to see the state they get into when left.'

'Oh, she'll be all right,' replied Sorley, and Alex laughed.

They drank down the drams and poured more. Sorley opened the stove's firebox and put in another peat.

'You cut peats the size of a bible, Alex. Heavy work that, you still at it?'

'Every summer, boy, you can't beat a day or two out on the moors when the sun's good and high in the sky. If you're still at home you'll come out again and do a bank with us?'

'Of course I will. I think about those days a lot when I'm sitting in the city looking out the window.'

'Well, the moor was full of people the last time you would have been on the peats. It's empty now, only myself and "The Weaver" still at it in this village. The oil killed people's interest in the peat, they're all too comfortable now, all in the comfort zone. Not even at the sheep much now, the fank has gone down so that it could be only one or two of us standing there now on a Saturday morning and it'll all be over by lunchtime now when it used to take a couple of weekends to do everybody's sheep.'

'Aye, but you don't get a good day out when the tanker comes, it's not the same,' said Sorley. 'Of course the television's done for a lot as well, sitting by the box in the corner instead of getting out.'

'This house used to be a great house for the peats. Your father would cut them by the ton and when we'd bring them home, well, this was the best house for a ceilidh. We'd all be sitting in around this kitchen and the windows would be open and some would be leaning in from the outside due to a lack of chair space inside, and even the old *cailleach* would take a nip that day. She was always glad to see the peats home.'

'I remember those days very clearly, it seems now like some kind of golden age,' said Sorley before recalling who it was he was talking to.

'Alex, sorry, I didn't mean to forget, or mention . . .'

'It's all right, son, we all remember that day at the peats very well and there's no point trying to forget it, you won't ever and still seems like yesterday. Do you remember, Sorley, how you ran out onto the moors that day after we brought Calum home? I remember all that commotion with Calum, and then your father out searching for you, thinking that maybe you had gone the same way as our boy, and then the day after that, too.'

'I do remember that day and night. I went to the river and the pool and stayed there – and how is Calum getting on now, how's the family?'

'Fine, just fine. I'll tell him you were asking after him. He's hoping to get back sometime but Canada's a long way away, especially with kids.'

Pouring another dram, Sorley clicked on the radio. A ceilidh was in full swing.

'The weather might not have changed since I was away, but the radio's still the best you can get!'

'For sure, and it reminds me of some of the nights we spent in this kitchen,' said Alex. 'Your father was never really one for the drams, but your mother would like to have a few folks in the house and a few drams was okay, think it helped her with the *cailleach* who'd sleep like a baby if she took even half a glass? She'd be quite happy sitting in the corner listening to the yarns.'

'Yes, and I remember the cove who used to stay looking in at the window through his cupped hands, he frightened us to death when we were kids.'

'I can't get his name, now, he was a brother to the wife's cousin, but he'd do no harm to anyone, never did, he was just a bit queer. They say the war did that to him.'

'His brother was the man who kept bees on the croft and I can remember him running out of the gate shouting: "The bees are swarming! The bees are swarming!" and my mother and father and all the children and other grown-ups came running out onto the road to try and follow the swarm. Some went with him out onto the moor, keeping the bees in sight as they flew, others went to try and watch the few trees there were around the houses to see if the bees took to a branch.

'Well, the bees made for the moor, but wherever they looked they could not find a place to settle. I remember that day. It was warm, bright and probably too hot for the bees in the hive, and we could see them swirling in a black ball, very clear against the blue sky, out over the moor and then flying this way and that. There were few trees on those hills, back then, and the bees just kept flying, not settling.

'He put a notice in the *Gazette* asking for the return of the bees if anyone saw them. Imagine it! A notice in the *Gazette*, cost him more than the bees were worth! Well, no one wrote, no one at all, and he couldn't afford to buy any more, so the hives just rotted away, and I remember that his net – the net he kept on his head when he was look-ing after those bees – sat on the gatepost from the day those bees swarmed to the day he died. The frame rusted, but he never took it in, and he never really thought that those bees had left the glen. Maybe they are out on the heather, and they'll come back to the hives soon, he would say – and that was just about all he talked about from then on, but for all his talk and fretting they never came back.'

A woman's voice came on the radio:

> An till mise chaoidh dha na glinn sa robh mi òg,
> Far 'm bu chridheil aoibhneach sinn gun uallach inntinn oirnn
> A bhuachchaillleachd chrodh-laoigh agus ghaimhne mar bu nòs
> An dùil an till mi chaoidh dha na glinn sa robh mo òg.

'That's a beautiful song that one,' said Alex, 'beautiful, and do you know the man that wrote that song was one of the ones who did get back.'

They finished their drams.

'Well, I must be going, the women will be wondering what's hap-pened to me,' said Alex, rising from his chair as he whistled to the dog and made to leave.

'Aye, I think they'll guess, and good to see you again,' said Sorley.

'Yes, and don't leave it so long next time,' added Alex, pressing Sorley to a promise that he'd call on them. The door was, as he had since learnt to say as second nature, 'always open'.

When Alex was gone and Sorley was alone again in the cottage, he went to bed but slept only until the first light of day woke him. He pulled back the curtain, a light was on in one of the houses down by the machair and the sight of it stopped him. It reminded him in its faint, isolated, melancholic glow of the last time he was on the island following the death of his father and he was staying in the nearby house of a cousin. He heard again the footfalls of the walk from the church to the cemetery the day they buried his father; the silences that surrounded the soft noise of leather-soled shoes on the loose shingle of the road. He could feel the discomfort of the cemetery's cold hand-shakes after the burial and see the lines of solemn black-suited men walking with the coffin, holding the blood-red cords that radiated from its brass handles. He could feel the weight of the coffin on his shoulders. The awkward changeovers, one man to another slowly, gently, wrestling the box from shoulder to shoulder, as they all took a turn beneath the coffin before it reached the cemetery gates.

There was the son, the nephew, the grandson, the best friend, the life-long neighbours all looking forlornly at the gaping ground. Men of the sea, many of them who, like his father, had struggled to make a living from the harvest of the waves; men who had grown strong in the face of the Atlantic. Men who had aged, the strength all but gone from their bodies, left with just enough to tend the sheep and peats and maybe grow potatoes in a corner of the croft.

In the cemetery, loved ones would stand eyeing the sand closing down around the coffin as it was lowered into the dark hole. Grown men, the sentimental dabbing of wet eyes with the corners of folded white hankies, burying their own.

When the coffin had been lowered to its final place and the words of the minister were finished, Sorley took up the shovel not leaving it to others. As he shovelled he sweated out the drink of the previous night, a thumping head distracting him from the task. The sudden work made him want to vomit, but he couldn't, not near the grave. He would fight it back in his throat and get on with the job as he bent down and lifted the sand, shovel after shovel onto the coffin like the tears that fell from his eyes.

The sand broke with a soft, dull thud on the clean, varnished coffin lid. He wept as the nameplate went from view and then the box was buried and then it was all over, and he was alone.

He joined the other men back at the house that day. Women in aprons greeted them all at the doorway. An efficient throng of kind ladies laying tables, serving soup from a large boiler on the gas and meat and vegetables from roasting dishes.

Whisky was shared out with the meals in small patterned glasses. Then one by one they went, leaving only the close family in the empty house.

Sorley had dreaded that funeral, all the questions, the probing, the fumbled answers. Most would remember him as a child and he was still *neònach*, more so than his brothers, he was the one that left, that went, that turned his back. He was the one who ran away as a child and as an adult.

Now that he was back, he'd face them all on a sunny spring day when things with Theresa had been resolved and maybe she would come back to him and live with him there on the island.

He got up and filled the kettle, trying to leave the memories behind. He raked over the clinkers in the firebox of the stove. A few of the small white coals still gave off a little heat that he could feel faintly on the back of his hand. They could stay in with the new fire.

He riddled out the ashes and binned them in a fold of newspaper. A coarse, sharp smell came from the white firelighter he lit and placed in the stove. He went outside for coal and wood. The northerly breeze was bitter with an icy chill. 'Snow's not far off now,' he thought.

The stove had taken only twenty minutes of his time to clean and fire-up. He had hoped it had taken an hour and that he was then that much nearer to the time when the post van might bring him a letter from Theresa.

He turned on the radio news to kill time until he felt able to go out on the moor. He'd walk that day where he couldn't be seen. It would be the same path he'd take today as he took yesterday: the old peat track that cut from behind the village across the moor. He'd find the derelict sheilings he once played in and he would rake through the grass that grew inside their half-fallen walls, searching for the remains of a rusted stove or a wine bottle. And always there would be rusted lager tins with faded pictures of '70s models in hot pants.

A few of the sheilings on the peat lands above the village had been restored, mostly by retired townfolk wanting to recover memories of the last childhood summer holidays spent on these moors.

Onto the moors they would come for six weeks in the height of summer in search of good pasture for the cattle – mothers and fathers, a milking cow, fishing rods, all sharing that one small space.

A few older stone sheilings remained further out on the moor, close to the edges of the many small lochs or on flat green swathes on sharp bends, all mostly derelict now, except for the chimney stacks and gable ends that stand firm against the weather over countless years.

Here too there remained little sign of cultivation, few signs to explain the abundance of small stone buildings that were then and now in the middle of nowhere.

Once the island's interior would have been thronged with cattle grazing and sheep huddled in every fold of the land. Men would be at the lochs hoping for trout, or better, salmon from the rivers. Sorley recalled the endless walking that accompanied a day at the lochs with his father, towing the otter board and its short string of ten flies through the water, experiencing the occasional shake and tug on the line as maybe two or three fish rose to the flies at once - hauling and man-handling the line, wet on the hands.

Then unhook and bag the catch and the walking would begin again, the nose of the board see-sawing out towards the centre of the loch, where, when the line was fully extended, it would swim like an exhausted black dog, fighting the current, the lead weight on its belly pulling it down but its head just above the waterline.

The radio quietly chatted of news from the city, traffic reports from places where they had daily hold-ups, weather, politicians, murder, sport; all of it stuff from the big cities. Down south the rain had brought more flooding. Pub and restaurant owners jabbering endless talk about financial ruin.

He put on his greatcoat. His boots were cold but he pulled them straight on and tied the laces twice round. He opened the door and started out into the breeze and the fierce cold drizzle that had started to fall. The road was soaked and glinted a dark shining slate-grey. The wind intensified the cold and drew his strength. He panted deeply as he reached the first summit on the moorland and the sharp edge of the wind told him that winter was close at hand.

The surrounding hills weren't visible; they hunched, shrouded in mist clouds. Sheep eyed him curiously as he walked on – a heavy figure in a dark coat, gradually disappearing into the mist. Unseen in the clouds, the droning engines of a distant helicopter could be heard, ferrying salmon smolts to fish cages on the distant lochs.

Many ghosts stalked that peat road and he was sure that many folk living in the small village thought that he was one of them. A dark figure heading out on the stony, rutted road made by carts and tractors many years ago, and before their time by feet alone.

The walker was alone in his determined stride, no dog at his side. Walking out in all weathers. Walking on ice or in the small burns that flowed down the broken track after heavy rain. He would walk to the top of the first rise of the moor, always stop there for a moment, and then walk on, out of view over the brow of the hill.

Up there he was with the ghosts of those who broke-in this land, who cut the first peat banks, who had lifted and turned peat for five hundred summers on this moor. He walked with those who had led their cattle on fine spring days out to good pasture on the moor. But no track went beyond the last line of peat banks. From there on, on this side of the village, the moor was untouched, uncut, a haunt of dunlin and of soaring buzzards; a land of rivers and low-banked lochs, where the air is shivered by the curlew's wailing call, and where the drumming of snipe eddies the humid summer air. A land where the cold blood call of the northern diver rises from beyond the loch shallows and where in spring the white sculptured heads of lobelia, solitary souls, nod towards the deeps.

From the brow of the hill you can see the gravedigger working slowly in the cemetery down by the shore. Keeping the grass short. Digging a lay at short notice and in all weathers. Plastic grass at the graveside, rolled out. Planks. Rope. Spade. Sand and soil.

Whenever the storms came the gravedigger would gather dead seabirds from the flanks of the machair. His father had done that job when Sorley was a boy and whenever he could he would bring a bird home for his supper, and always said he preferred oystercatcher to chicken.

Later that afternoon, Sorley sat once again in the armchair in the kitchen, peering through the small window out at the road. The post van had driven out beyond the houses by the shore and had continued in to the nearest house along the road to his own. The postman dropped letters into his neighbour's house and returned to the small red van. Sorley watched as he turned it in the driveway and drove back to the shore, away from the cottage.

There was no going back. He was living on the island now. He would live far from Theresa and the home they had made together in the city. He would be alone in the home he knew as a child. The home he once left for the allure of the city.

He put his coat back on and left the cottage, closing the door behind him, and walked towards the phone box. He felt for loose change in the pocket of his coat, and pulled out a small handful. He walked on but in the knowledge that he could not bring himself to call Theresa. He was not ready to speak to her. He knew she was angry and hurt and that she thought that he had deserted her for the pursuit of a whim, something that was beyond her comprehension. But he walked on and as he walked so he could feel the first tears moisten the corners of his eyes, and when the salt tear grew heavy it ran slowly down his cheek, and others ran behind it. He was walking and crying. Crying bitterly, alone on the road in the half-light. Nobody else walked that road at night and so he walked on, turning away from the path that led to the phone box and on towards the shore and the low walls of the ruined chapel.

A curlew broke cover in front of him, forsaking its hiding place among the grass-covered stones of a long-fallen house and as it went out towards the old *feannagan* in the neighbouring village, so it smattered the cold grey evening air with the glint of its ghost call.

Sorley sat in the armchair and the radio played. The pale white light from the old neon strip on the kitchen ceiling filled the small, warm room. The year was nearly out.

Snow had been falling most of that day but between the showers the cloud revealed a brilliant, bright blue sky and vivid white sun, and when the sky had cleared the sea settled and the white light of the day would flood the kitchen and the neon glow was drowned in that profusion.

The mainland mountains emerged from behind the clouds as diamonds set in the land, their jagged forms razor sharp against the sky before the clouds would close in again and snow would fall and the squalls would torment the ocean and the neon glow in the kitchen would return as though it had risen for breath from beneath those waves.

The Highlands and Islands news came on the radio and the first item woke Sorley from his slumbers in the armchair.

'A rescue is underway for a climber from Glasgow who failed to return overnight to his hotel,' said the newsreader.

By the time of the mid-afternoon bulletins that regular phrase had hardened to the headline that the search for the missing climber had been called off for the day due to bad weather conditions – and the climber was named as Danny MacDonald, a Glasgow man who was an experienced climber.

Sorley knew at once that he must phone Grace. It was Danny who was missing in the wilderness he loved. Sorley rose from the armchair, frantic, but trying to stay calm. He put on his greatcoat and boots. He grabbed more change from the pile on the kitchen table, opened the front door and was gripped by the bitter coldness. He started the walk towards the faint yellow glow of light within the red phone box that was situated at the end of a lane near to the neighbouring village. As he walked, his boots sank into the deep snow, the coldness covering his ankles.

Sorley reached the phone box and dialled Theresa's number. He had not spoken to her since he left their flat in the city but now he had to, and he felt also that the time that had elapsed between their talking was, in the circumstance, nothing in comparison to the tragedy he feared was unfolding in the mountains. He felt that they belonged together and he had to talk to her now. She would, he thought, be expecting him to call.

The line connected but Theresa's phone was engaged. A formal-sounding voice came on the line: 'please hold the line, the person you are calling knows you are waiting'.

'Theresa,' said Sorley, 'it's me. I just heard the news about Danny. It was on the radio. I'll call later. Tell Grace I called and I'm thinking of her and praying for Danny.'

He put the phone down, picked up the change he had not used from the top of the coin box and left the warmth of the small box.

He walked back towards the cottage, frustrated at not being able to speak to Theresa and he could not believe that he had said that he was 'praying' for Danny. How innane, he thought, how hopeless. He wanted to walk back to the phone and leave another message, apologising for what he had said but he would not. He did not want to make his own thoughts the centre of their consideration at the time they would be desperately worried for Danny.

Sorley stopped on the road and looked again towards the mainland mountains, the wilderness of snow and rock and bitter wind, and he thought of where Danny might be that night. Was he lying at the bottom of a gully, his body contorted to the harsh shape of a boulder? Was he alive even, sheltering in a snow hole, waiting for the conditions to improve before making his move for safety? But no, Sorley's instincts told him that was not the truth.

Was he cradled in the branches of a silver birch or a rowan growing beneath a sheer slope? Sorley saw Danny then, saw his body held in the branches of the tree. His head was hanging down, his eyes were open, facing the blue sky, and his mouth was open as though he were singing but he was silent. Maybe there was a slight movement in his eyes. The eyes were moving as though surveying the glens and the sky but they did not show signs of panic or fear or pain.

Sorley tried to close the thoughts out of his mind and pulled the collar of his coat up around his neck and walked on, not turning again to look at the mountains. As he walked, the snow started falling. The flakes were cold against his face and then they fell faster and his breathing became tight and panicked.

When he came close to the cottage he ran the last few steps to the door and pushed it open with force as though there were a heavy weight on the other side. He entered and shook the snow from his boots and coat. The radio was still on. The heat from the stove hit him and he felt drained of energy. He sat in the armchair, his feet up on the stove rail.

The radio talked on but Sorley was not listening. Intermittently, between the snow showers, the beam of the lighthouse came into the kitchen.

Sorley looked out towards the snowfields. He looked towards the mountains, no longer visible. He looked towards the sea and conjured the sound of waves breaking on the snow-covered shore and he saw Danny's body lying there. If only he could banish these visions from his mind.

Sorley woke. He had been sleeping in the armchair. It was nearly ten o'clock and still snowing. He sat dazed and absent-minded for a moment and then the reality of the day returned to him. He had to phone Theresa again. He put back on the boots and the heavy dark coat. He opened the door and was now confronted by a white blast as the snow blew in on the force of the gale. The streetlamp at the junction of the crossroads in the village was only faintly visible, but its dull glow illuminated a thick torrent of snow falling to the ground.

'God help him,' said Sorley under his breath as he was suddenly struck by thoughts of how violent the conditions must be on the high slopes of the mountains. The snow was now knee-deep with drifts even deeper and Sorley's progress into the gale was slow. As he walked his face was whipped by shards of ice that fell with the snow. The temperature was falling and the hard granular snow blew like desert sand in the high wind. Sorley knew that the walk to the phone was treacherous, foolish even, and that Theresa would not have expected him to call that night. But he kept on, kept on through fear and sorrow.

He reached the phone box, opened the door and almost fell into the light-filled space. He was then out of the wind but stationary and he could feel that the chill that had gone into his bones.

He placed change on the top of the coin box. He lifted the receiver and dialled Theresa's number.

The phone began to ring and Sorley was suddenly anxious and panicking about how he would speak to Theresa, what he would say after all the time that had passed without them talking. He put the receiver down and then stood shivering in the phone box.

He picked up the change and placed it in his pocket and pushed against the phone box door. But as he did so the phone rang. He looked at it, startled. He had not contemplated that possibility. He placed a hand on the receiver but did not pick it up. He waited and it rang and rang under his hand until, finally, he lifted it and slowly brought it to his ear.

'Hello,' he said.

'Hello. Somebody there called this number, this is Theresa MacRath.'

Sorley realised that she had not recognised his voice.

'Theresa, it's Sorley.'

'Sorley,' she said quietly, but a little surprised.

'I heard about Danny and wanted to phone you. I called earlier.'

'Yes, I know, I got the message.'

'How's Grace?'

'Devastated, trying to keep calm.'

'And how are you?'

'Trying to hold myself together, for Grace, really.'

'Will you tell her that I'm thinking of her?'

'Yes, I will.'

'Is she with you now?'

'Yes, but she's sleeping. She had a tablet and finally slept.'

'Well, I won't wake her.'

'No.'

'If there's anything I could do, I'd do it.'

'I know, Sorley, but we all just have to sit and wait. The police say the search will resume at first light.'

'The weather's atrocious here.'

'And here.'

'God help him out there. He was experienced enough though, if anyone will know what to do he will.'

'Yes, we've not given up hope yet, but it's looking bad. The police have warned us that his chances of survival in these conditions are very slight.'

'I'll call you tomorrow?'

'Yes, we'd like that.'

'Take care and give my love to Grace and tell her that I'm thinking of her.'

'Okay. We'll speak tomorrow.'

Sorley replaced the receiver and felt a wave of relief flow through his body. He pushed against the phone box door and started the walk for home.

When he made it back to the cottage he went straight to bed. He was shivering with cold but could not sleep for thoughts of Danny racing through his mind, Danny out there in the mountains on such a night. He would be near An Teallach, the mountain that Sorley could see from his kitchen window on a clear day, but seemed to be on the other side of the universe, remote from them all.

The following day was brilliant white and no more snow had fallen. The cold of night stayed around the house, hard as stone. Sorley went out to the peat stack and took a bucketful from the warm interior of the mound, his frozen hands delving blindly inside, searching for the black peat with which he could re-light the stove.

The north wind rose and fell and with each blow it sculpted razor-sharp angles on the top of the waist-deep drifts, cutting ice curls in the low, white summits.

Sorley's teeth chattered and his hands ached with the pain of cold that had grown in them. Above the moorland the sky was pale blue, bleached almost white, and Sorley knew from the colour that more snow would come in the time before darkness descended again.

The snow would come from pink or even orange-toned clouds that would roll from the northern horizon and blacken the sky until a white veil would draw beneath them and the snow would fall and then it would pass over, leaving silence on a newly covered Earth.

He turned towards the east and saw that the day was clear and in the almost pristine visibility he saw An Teallach on the horizon, its open arms reaching to him. The mountain glowed with snow, pale blue, before the clouds enclosed it once again, and Sorley thought again of Danny.

He carried the pail into the kitchen and threw a few *caoran* onto an orange-flaming firelighter and shut the small blue doors of the stove, enclosing the orange glow.

He sat back into the armchair but he could not settle as pictures of Danny injured in the mountains, maybe sheltering in a snow hole, dominated his mind. He walked the floor, back and forth and then, desperate to gain some calmness he reached up to the mantle shelf, his finger groping for the cold touch of the whisky bottle he kept there. Sorley unscrewed the top and drank slowly, a large mouthful, its taste sharp in his mouth. His other hand reached over to the fat round knob on the top of the radio and it turned, clicking the radio into life and crackling as he found the right volume.

Gaelic songs filled the room from the radio and Sorley sat drinking until his head was heavy and he slipped in and out of sleep, tired enough to fall deeply asleep, yet too drunk to remain awake.

Daylight was leaving the sky when he finally rose from the armchair and turned on the neon strip light. A yellow, bleaching flood of light filled the kitchen and took the remaining light from the day, bringing blackness to the window, and with it a reflection of himself.

Sorley looked deep into the image reflected there: his face was almost covered in a coarse, auburn beard, his hair ruffled, his eyes deep set in their sockets and exaggerated by black lines that ringed their base. He looked wild and in the yellow light, pale and drawn beyond his years. His clothes looked shabby and loose with wear.

Sorley drank again, trying not to focus on the image floating in the darkness of the window; the winter mirror that clad the windows with introspection.

He thought of Danny on An Teallach, he thought of the body hanging in the ice cornice, his open mouth frozen in a final, falling cadence of terror. Sorley felt powerless but he knew . . . had he not once brought Calum back, and in the cave had he not seen how Angus saved a child, and was saved himself? He could go for Danny, bring him back.

The Gaelic news came on the radio and Sorley heard that the search for the missing climber had been called off again for the day due to increasingly bad conditions in the Wester Ross area. The search would begin again at first light. The newscaster added that mountain rescue were still confident of finding the man alive as he was believed to be a competent and well-equipped climber with many years' experience in the mountains.

Sorley heard himself yelling at the radio, 'for God's sake keep going!', but he knew it was pointless to get frustrated, they would be doing everything possible, everything humanly possible.

He put on his coat and went to the end of the house and looked out at the mainland. He longed then for the boat and the shallow bay, the whalebone arches and the flight across the vast moorland and the white mountains. Yes, that flight. He yearned for that flight far inland. He yearned for the feeling of the wing muscles on his back so that he could again taste the warm, dark blood of the seal's liver, iron thick on his tongue; so that he could go to Danny.

He walked away from the house and then on past the church. Dark yellow light from its high windows flooded the surrounding snow-covered ground and he heard from within the sound of the Gaelic *Salm* and he thought of the people standing there, shoulder to shoulder. He longed for their surety, for the comfort of the psalms, the community of knowing.

Sorley returned home. He walked slowly, his eyes wet with the salt burn of the tears he had shed in loneliness. He was again in that familiar kitchen, looking out at his own image in the night-black window. The radio was on and he had before him on the sill, the opened bottle of whisky. The lighthouse beam swung beneath a low cloud, illuminating the sea nearest to the shore, and casting a white cloud of light into the cloud-thick sky.

His eyes focused through the window, out to a small, half-buried form nestled in a drift by the croft wall. Sorley could see the long beak that protruded from the small form of its head. He went out to the drift and there, frozen such that its wing feathers were brittle with the cold, was a snipe, almost perfect in death.

He remembered seeing the snipe probing at the moss-covered stones of that wall when he went for the peats earlier that morning. He had never seen them so close to the house before the snow had fallen that day, and he knew that the weather had forced them up from the saltings and from the moors. The snipe was, he thought, like himself, an isolated wanderer of the remote places. He carried the lifeless bird into the kitchen and placed it beside the fox head on the shelf above the stove.

He then stared out at the lighthouse beam, and he was a young boy again walking the peat road in early summer. It was evening and the sun had set, filling the sky with a wild bruise of red and gold, and above him the air shivered with a faint sound that came from an unseen source.

He thought that the sound was the true whistle that would bring forth the aurora, the *fir-chlis*, to the night sky. As he had stood looking into the summer sky, his head had arched back, and he had become aware that he was not alone on that road. From the moor, a figure, heavy and large in a dark, full-length cloth coat, had arrived and asked him what it was he was looking at.

'What is that?' he had asked the man.

'That's the *naosg*. It's a snipe, drumming the air through its wings. *Naosg* is the Gaelic for that bird, Sorley, and not many folk here know that now.'

And with that the old man, whom he knew well and who lived close by the end of their own croft, had walked on home, and he too was craning his neck to catch a sight of the drumming *naosg*.

Sorley remembered then the day, when he was still a young boy, that he had watched another snipe from that same kitchen window. He had heard it calling all that morning from somewhere close by on the moor. It called as though in agony, and standing with his father at the end of the house he had seen it through the field glasses, pacing the peat road, lagging a broken wing awkwardly from a shattered joint.

They walked towards it and saw how the hooded crows watched over its frantic meander from their perch on the fence wire. But his father would not let him take it home. When his father turned to go, the boy carried on past the snipe and the crows, and with tears in his eyes that he did not want his father to see, he reached the top of the hill. He sat for hours looking up at the white-topped outline of the far Sutherland Hills.

He watched as the crows, startled by the invasion of a bigger bird, suddenly flew from their high wire leaving the snipe to a violent death at the beak of a bonxie. The boy stood at the summit and watched as the skua rose and carried off its prey in its beak. The snipe's wings were still flapping as the skua went beyond his sight out over the moorland towards the sea.

The radio played on almost silently in the kitchen.

He put the bottle to his lips and drank deeply, and the whisky made its path through his throat and into the hollow pit of his stomach. He stood at the window watching the lighthouse beam circle the shore and the low rolling hills of *Rubha*, and then open onto the sea in the bay.

Pibroch came from the radio and as the notes slowly stepped from the chanter Sorley thought of the cave and the stones, he thought of Danny in the mountains and of Mary lying in the bay, her mind fevered by her journeying.

Sorley thought, too, of Donald in his weakness, and the choking boy who would soon stay beside Mary's drowned body. Sorley knew that he was the last of their line. Mary, Angus, Morag, Sorley. Mary, Angus, Morag, Sorley. He repeated the names again and again in his head.

Sorley put on his coat and held the whisky bottle in the long side pocket. Low clouds hung over the moor as he walked the peat road, past the place where the snipe once paced, and onto the low summit of Druim Reidh. He looked out at the sea and saw there, at the machair, the remains of St Aula's, its roof open to the sky. He turned and walked out onto the moorland. The moor was silent save for the sound of the distant river.

He yearned for the plover that in spring had called to him, and for the stonechats that clattered their song as they led him out onto the moors. Snow clung to the dead heather, and sheet ice crackled under his feet as he walked. He stopped and drank from the bottle, and then walked on, cutting across the moorland towards the river until he was at the pool where Calum had drowned.

Before him was the stunted birch tree, its crown of branches cut and funnelled by the wind. His hands traced the bark until he found the wounds where he'd carved the names. A torrent of peat-brown water rushed over the falls at the top end of the pool, and Sorley sat on the lowest boulder.

He pulled his buttoned coat up to cover his head, and he heard the river water falling on stones. The visions after the beating, the flight, the stones, these things had brought him back to the island. Or maybe it was his grandmother calling him back, calling for the gift to be reborn. And what use were these gifts if he could not now prove their value?

He'd come to the island because of what he knew. He could no longer live where he was not wanted, where his gifts were not wanted. The shaman must be alone.

He'd seen in the cave the journey taken by Mary. He'd seen Angus save a child and he had saved a child himself and he now was the inheritor of that *taghairm*. Chosen, maybe, but with certainty the inheritor. He'd argued with Theresa and maybe now he had the chance to show her that he was not mad or insane, that the fox and the deer bone were natural to his cause. He'd show her. He'd bring Danny back to them.

The words in his head sounded ridiculous in their indignation as he heard them. How would he go to Danny? All the journeys he had made before to the other land, the land of ice and mountains, the land of the spirits, of the past, had been almost as if he were a traveller, a mere visitor, not one who comes with a task to perform, a goal to achieve. He was a novice, wounded by events, weak, yes weaker than them all, but this was the next big step.

He had inherited the gift; he had been chosen and initiated into a world far beyond his preconceptions of the powers and meaning of that gift. He had a task that was more compelling and difficult than the mere visions experienced by his grandmother. He had been shown episodes of the lives of others with that gift, others in his bloodline who had travelled this way before. Yes, that was it, others had travelled this way before, others had gone to the same places and that was all they knew, that is all you need to know, how to go there, how to get back.

Now, after many years, that power was needed, full force. The power to rescue the spirit of one who has died and to return it to the body it left behind. The final act would be the séance of the *taghairm*, perhaps the last time he or anyone else would call upon its power. Angus's gift would be followed, Angus's knowledge recalled.

He went back to the cottage and turned the radio on to listen to the news. The items came and went, national, international, local but this morning there was no mention of the climber lost in the mountains. Danny's story had slowly dropped down the news agenda and then, that morning, had finally disappeared from the bulletins. Danny's fate had been sealed, it seemed; the search was off. Whether his body returned or not was now up to the providence of nature, and the ill-fortune of some other climber to come across his remains.

Sorley went to the window and looked out across the Minch toward the point on the mainland where he knew An Teallach was hidden behind a sheet of white cloud. The raw sorrow and shock that he had felt when first he knew that Danny was missing had left his mind now. He felt numb, useless in the face of events, for sure, but his own sorrows felt as nothing save for the fact that his future depended on him bringing Danny back.

He would find Danny. He would go to him. Not to the mountain where he lay dead, but to the place where his spirit had gone. He would bring his spirit back and Danny would live again.

Sorley took the fox skull from the shelf and caressed its fragile bones. He wanted to journey once again, fly above the city and in the dark night he wanted to lie again with the fox in its hole beneath the ground, the frozen ground. He wanted the fox beside him as he walked to the cave. He yearned for the railway banks, the dark night of the burial. He yearned for the gift to have value once again.

The following day, his leather greatcoat for a hide, Sorley walked out towards the falls on the river. Snowmelt had fed the river's torrent beyond bursting point and its lower meanders flooded the salt marshes. A bitter wind blew from the mainland where the mountains shone white against the winter sky.

The peat road led him out beyond the last house in the village. Before him the signs of the old settlements by the river came into view, the runrigs on the hills above the riverbanks, the fallen stones of old dwellings, the paths that led to places not now used by man.

The moor was silent save for the distant roar of river water. There was no calling of birds, no cawing of crows. The wren's song did not that day shiver the air but he felt its presence, felt its eyes watching him. The birds too had gone to ground and stayed there in silence as he walked on towards the river.

Sorley reached the pool by the falls. A torrent of peat-brown water gushed from its rocky aperture, smashing the pool water. The flat, table-like ledge beside the falls, where the stones had shown him Mary and Angus had lain, was covered in bare heather. Ice clung between the twists of the heather's dark stems.

Above the pool on the banks beside the falls stood the birch tree, its bark carved with names. Sorley climbed the bank and stood beneath the branches of the tree. He looked up at its crown and its height seemed to have grown rapidly such that it reached towards the low clouds and perhaps beyond into the clear sky.

He cupped his hands about its trunk and began to climb. Slowly he rose into its bottom branches climbing awkwardly through the mass of thin, purple-brown twigs. As he gained height the far mainland mountains came into full view. His eyes were level with their snow-covered summits and he could see beyond them into a plain of peaks and ridges that stretched beyond the curve of the earth. Above his head, indifferent crows perched in the branches speaking noisily to each other as though engaged in some agitated argument about his visit. They let him pass and he climbed on until they were below his feet, clear of his eyes, clear of his hands, and each was a spirit, each an escapee, indifferent to the lives of men. Each had spoken and seen and heard the things of men, and each had flown on black wings where he had flown.

Sorley stopped climbing and turned to face the sea and the land. Far below, beneath his feet, the windows of the houses of the village shimmered with faint light and smoke rose from their chimneys. He could see that a few of the villagers had gathered on the road and stood staring out at him as he climbed, but they did not disturb him, did not stop him. One of them whistled through his fingers, a shrill, constant whistle.

Sorley gripped the birch trunk with his legs and opened out his arms.

On the ground, they saw him silhouetted against the sky, a distant figure, high in the branches of the birch by the falls. He did not fly, did not glide on wings, but stayed motionless and listened to the wind and the chatter of the crows; listened to the roar of the falls and waited for word of Danny.

As darkness fell so Sorley descended the birch. By the dark pool he opened out his coat and lay on the ground wrapping it around his body and head until he had closed out all light, closed out the day.

The torrent of the falls filled his head, its rushing force took shape as rhythm, constant, slow rhythm that shook and rippled through the riverbank and through his body. The soft ground beneath the heather slowly opened for him and he sank into its fold, a silvered, buried boulder a pillow for his head until his wings opened and he flew from the riverbank out over the ocean towards the hills.

He soared above the plain of peaks and on towards the shallow bay, the mountains and the cave and in the branches of a tree close by he found Danny.

Sorley went to him but Danny did not engage with him. Sorley grabbed at his shoulders and tried to pull him from the branches, but he would not come.

Sorley asked him to return but Danny shook his head. Sorley asked him again but he gave no reply, and when he asked him why he would not come back, Danny did not speak a word and then in silence Sorley left and wandered in the hills, deep snow muffling his footsteps. Danny would not return; he wanted to remain there, Sorley could not save him.

Sorley was aware of the biting coldness of the ground and the waterfall deafened him. He threw open the coat and saw that it was nighttime and he was not sure if he had been there for a day or a week. The sky had cleared and he walked back to the village aware that behind the house windows, eyes were watching him on the road.

In the cottage, he sat in the chair by the stove. Its flame was out and the metal plates icy cold. He did not light it but sat shivering in the chair. He had not considered the possibility that Danny would not come back with him. He had not thought that possible. He had failed; he had gone to him and had failed to bring him back. He had not the power to retrieve him, could not overpower his will. In his mind he saw himself stripping bark from the birch tree, stripping off the names he carved there, stripping off all trace of what had gone before until the trunk was white and naked as weathered bone.

Sorley knew that it was the end. The cottage seemed bare and the fox skull only bodily remains, cold in his hands.

He started to walk to the phone box to call Theresa and Grace. He'd tell them that he tried to retrieve Danny, tried to bring him back but as he thought of the words he felt ashamed. How could he tell them that? What if he inherited the gift, its powers were not strong in him and with this and all other failures, he would live in torment.

The following morning, Sorley put on his suit and the fine old shoes he wore for weddings and funerals and went into town. There he drifted from bar to bar until in the afternoon he was reduced to staggering through their half-open doorways and resting against town walls. He drifted on until he was refused drink and then he walked as best he could towards the bus station, folding one foot over the other as he went along the street. He went into the town's small off-licence and managed to buy a bottle of whisky.

He arrived at the bus station and knew then that he would not be going home. He would go to the far north, to the cold, dark harbour in the northernmost village on the island. He would go to the sea and there he would plead for his own spirit and the spirits of Mary and Angus. He would plead for Danny. He would plead to the old God of the ocean that once gave life and abundance, and yet was capable of unimaginable cruelty.

The journey north was rapid, the road cutting across a vast, open land, a land of bogs and bog candles, of the brackish water of countless shallow lochans. He saw it all as the bus hurtled past.

Occasionally, the driver, who he did not know but who seemed to know him and his every move over the majority of his life, turned and spoke to him from behind the shuttered cabin at the front. But Sorley could not reply and then, when he could think of no new platitudes, he kept his face fixed firmly in a gaze towards the moorland.

Eventually, the bus pulled to a halt at the top of the path that led down to the beach and the harbour by the squat houses that seemed always to be in darkness. He could hear the roar of the ocean waves as they broke on the expanse of yellow sand that stretched before him and the harbour wall held a pocket of calmness in its heart, bracing the elements.

Far out, a solan goose rose into the twilight and dived on tucked wings towards a pinpoint in the sea.

Blathering and angry Sorley MacRath strides out into the waves. The fading grey light of evening coddles the ocean as it breaks over the northern shores of the island and over his tan brogues, his suit trousers and the vents of his jacket.

In his right hand he holds a half-finished bottle of whisky that shakes with the tightness of his grip about its neck. His left hand fists at the sky as he yells at the invisible spirit of the deep.

'Shony you fuck, I'll give you drink! I'll give you drink and what will you give me? Come on, what's keeping you? Answer me! Come on you fuck, lost your tongue, ah, Shony?'

He is then silent with the whisky bottle lowered forlornly at his side as the coldness of the salt seawater cuts into his bones. The sap has fallen from his throat and only the sound of the waves and the coarse, calling grate of gulls hangs in the air.

The gulls hover in the low reaches of the darkening sky, motionless on outstretched wings held aloft by the force of the Atlantic gale. Some follow behind him as he walks out into the ocean, his coat flapping in the wind like the ruddy sail of an old boat setting out into the rolling currents of the high seas.

'Here, take it all!' he suddenly shouts, rejuvenated as he pours the remains of the whisky into the ocean.

'Take all I've left!' he shouts as he throws the empty whisky bottle far out into the waves.

He wades on into the sea and as he walks he becomes aware that he is being followed. He turns and sees a small boy and a woman behind him, and others join them. Their faces are familiar, he's seen them before, perhaps he loved them, knew them once; maybe some of them he has known only as names from the past.

'Go back!' he yells to them. 'Leave me to it! Go back in for Christ's sake, go back in!'

But even as he shouts back at them he knows that it is too late, they've gone and the gulls' call is no longer a processional but a siren of his anxieties, a relentless call across the elements – the land and sea and sky.

As the waves rise up around his chest and neck his steps become uncertain and his progress slows such that he is barely moving against the force of water that pushes him back to the shore.

He turns once more and sees a huddle of people staring at him from the harbour wall; some are waving to him, others are calling his name, but he pays no heed to their frantic shouts and faces out towards the ocean once more.

At last the waves break their soft salt over his face and he can taste their waters in his mouth. His eyes feel the chill of the north Atlantic and he ducks his head below the surface and down into the darkness and silence that the seabed quietly clutches. His feet can no longer touch the floor and the strong current carries him back and forth as he floats in the glaucous hue of the ocean.

By chance, he surfaces for a moment and for the last time sees the gannets circling above him before they dive into the sea not far off, and then he is under again and far removed from land, unconscious, drifting in the waves.

FIVE

Sorley wakes, wakes in an unfamiliar bed with the pain of bright lights in his eyes. He's alone in a single room.

A nurse enters the room.

'Where am I?' he asks in a thin, weak voice.

'Where do you think? You're in hospital, you're lucky to be alive,' she responds.

'Yes, lucky to be alive. I guess I am. How did I get here?'

'In an ambulance.'

'Oh, when was that?'

'Last night, you were pulled from the sea. Is there anyone you want me to contact for you?'

'No, I've only myself. Am I hurt, badly hurt?'

'Some cuts to the legs, nothing serious, your heart was failing, maybe hypothermia, but rest now, the doctor will be in to see you. Do you feel like trying that again?'

'No.'

'You were drinking heavily,' she said, taking his blood pressure.

'Yes, I suppose I was.'

'We'll have to keep an eye on you. Can I get you anything?'

'No, not now, I'm fine.'

'Your pressure seems to be settling down now.'

'Good.'

'Do you feel cold at all, any numbness?'

'No.'

'Your face is bruised.'

'Oh.'

'Nothing serious, it'll take a week to go down. The drip will stay in for another day, if everything else is okay.'

Sorley rested his head back on the pillow; he hadn't noticed the drip, feeding into his lower arm through a length of plastic and sticking plaster. His head ached, thumping violently if he lifted it too far. Thoughts of Danny came back to him, but fleetingly he knew it was too late now, that it was over.

'Let me take your pulse,' the nurse said, lifting his wrist.

'Maybe some fluctuations, they might settle down. A psychiatrist will be in tomorrow, ask you a few questions about how you're feeling and how you came to be here.'

'Okay, good, thanks.'

'What happened that day, in the morning?'

'Nothing, I was just stressed, I suppose. My brother-in-law is lost on the mountains, over the water there; it's been on the news. I started to drink.'

'I'm sorry for that.'

'Have you heard anything, any news?'

'No, sorry, I'll try and find out.'

The nurse left the room. Sorley felt exhausted, depressed; he was back at the beginning, and back where the fight had left him, only now he was alone. He'd endure a few days in the hospital, play the game until he could get out and get back to the cottage, get straight.

In the morning, the doctor did his rounds. His manner was aloof, disdainful of Sorley's problems but his recovery was noted and he would be moved to another ward if the psychiatrist wanted him to stay.

After lunch he dozed but woke to the sound of a newspaper being folded, close by. He opened his eyes.

'Hello, Sorley.'

'Alex.'

'Sorry for your troubles, Sorley. How are you feeling?'

'Tired and a bit foolish.'

'Don't worry, son, everyone's thinking about you. We want you to get well and out of here. How long are they keeping you?'

'Don't know yet. I was hoping to get out tomorrow but they've a lot of questions to ask. But everything else seems to be fine. I'm alive, breathing, I can't ask for more than that just now.'

'No, that's right, you won't get far without those two. Well, take your time, there's no point hurrying anything, have a rest for a few days. You were lucky they pulled you out.'

'Yes, I suppose I was. Who was it?'

'A local man, saw you from the shore and went in after you. They had the helicopter down on the beach within a few minutes.'

'Shit.'

'Look, I don't want to force you or anything, but if you ever need to talk, Sorley, if we can help, you can always talk to us.'

'I know, Alex, it's been a bad few months, but I want to come through it now.'

'Won't be long before we're back at the peats.'

'No, not long now.'

'I was thinking of going out this weekend, have a look at the area, the banks, see how they over-wintered.'

'You'll have yours first home again, Alex, can't have you coming second.'

'Well, you can't rely on the summers now, not as hot as they were in my day, so you need as much time out there as you can get.'

Finally, the psychiatrist came to the ward. He held a file of notes: some new coloured pages at the front with scrawled handwriting, charts between the pages, and older pages, some crossed through in pencil at the back.

The questioning was direct, to the point. Did he want to kill himself? What was his mood? Had he tried to kill himself before? Endless dissection of that moment and all roads led to that moment but he could not speak of his flight, could not speak of his failure, of his ambition to save a dead man, save himself, save what remained with Theresa. Those words, those thoughts would trap him there, best keep them in.

Trauma, post-coma trauma – that was a way out. What about drink, shall I tell you of my fantasies of other-worldly power? I can take control, you see, can bring someone back from the dead like they used to, way back, can conjure with myth and magic, and then he stopped. Sorley stopped his thoughts from racing, stopped the anger and frustration and rested.

He was going home, he was okay. They'd call and see him every week, once a week for six weeks for an hour, a nurse, a man if he wanted, or he could go to them, for lunch, the day room and he could call at any time. If he felt like harming himself, just call the ward.

Thank you. Thank you, he said, going home in borrowed clothes. No sign of the suit, no sign of the brogues.

Back in the kitchen, back in the armchair, back with the radio and the neon glow and the night-black window and the lighthouse beam. Pibroch and bird song, the fox skull and the *naosg*, both stiff as stone.

Saturday morning and Alex came to the door, a spade in his hand and the dog pacing anxious with expectation at his feet. The day was cold and bright with the brilliant yellow light of a distant sun but diamond-edged with the freshness of a northerly wind, a clinical light. They walked up the old peat road, the dog running on. Ice sheets covered the pot-holes in the road and beneath their white surfaces cold meltwater ran in rivulets, cutting clear-lined patterns, and the frozen gravel crunched beneath their feet.

'I sat most Saturdays this winter in my kitchen looking out this way, waiting for the weather to improve and the spring to come,' said Alex, 'waiting to get out here again.'

'Aye, you can't beat it,' replied Sorley, stopping on the path for a moment and turning back to face the village. The snow-covered mass of An Teallach dominated the distant horizon.

'Terrible what happened to your brother-in-law,' said Alex, breaking into Sorley's fixed stare. 'They might have got to him if the weather had lifted even for a few hours.'

'I'm not so sure he would have wanted to come back, it's how he wanted to go, what he loved doing.'

'I saw in the paper they found his remains and brought him down.'

'Yes, he'd fallen.'

They turned to walk on, the dog was standing ahead of them on the road, its eyes and tail pleading for them to catch him up and they walked on the short distance to where a path led down the hillside toward the river and went into the area of the peat-banks.

'That's your own peat-banks there, Sorley,' said Alex, pointing at a fallen row. 'The weather's undercut the faces now, but they were good peats in their day.'

'Burnt hot, my mother used to say, great for starting the fire in the morning but you'd get through buckets of them in a day,' replied Sorley.

'Let's see how these have done this winter,' said Alex, walking the short distance over to his own peat-banks.

Sorley looked at the faces of Alex's banks: they gleamed, smooth, almost black with barely a few small, open, drier gashes where the wind had opened a minor fracture in the surface.

'Looking good, Alex,' said Sorley.

'Yes, they're fine but I'll be cutting less this year, we'll do a few loads and you can get a load for your stove, if you're staying for the summer.'

'Yes, I will be, I think.'

Neither spoke then, letting Sorley's acknowledgement linger.

When their work at the peat-banks was done they started back up the path towards the village, but Sorley remained, letting Alex and the dog go on back before him – he'd walk on upwards. He reached the summit of the hills above the moor at the back of the village.

At the top, he disturbed a large black crow that flew off, away across the moor, cawing back at home, but he did not reply. He looked out over the Minch towards the mainland mountains, and then north at the rolling moorland hills and the watery blue sky. The river cut a course between the two, its roar faintly audible to him and he could hear a slow rhythm in its movement and he focused on its drone.

He was calm then, his mind had emptied as he walked that path and listened to the river, and he realised that for the first time since he returned to the island he saw and felt nothing in that empty landscape, no yearning, no struggle, no sorrow. He wanted to be nothing but a part of its movement, its emptiness and its presence.

That night, the cloudless, moonless sky was full of stars and Sorley stood at the back door to the cottage, his neck craned upwards. The aurora flickered low in the northern sky and from beyond the croft came an occasional billow from curlew or plover that mingled with the sound of the still roaring river. He did not want the wings for flight, or the cave or the bay or the boat; as he looked at the night sky he knew that this being was enough and the great flight would come by watching, listening, remaining, and they would be the gifts he kept.

Glossary and Notes

A bheil duine an seo? Is anyone in?

airigh, a 'sheiling' or small cottage on the moors often used for weeks at a time by a family when taking cattle out to fresh pastures

A' chaitheamh, consumption, tuberculosis

an Sgarbh, cormorant

an tobar, a well

barrad (bàrr-fàd), the top layer of peat in the peat bank

bàrr na sgeine, the top edge of the *tairsgeir* blade

Breabadair Diluain, literally 'a Monday Weaver', the phrase was used for those who could not be punished on the Sabbath as such activity was not in keeping with Sabbath Law, but would get it the following day!

broinn, the floor in front of the peat bank

cailleach, an old woman

caoran, small peats, most often crumbled; very dry black peat

*carcair, Dwelly's Illustrated Gaelic to English Dictionary (Birlinn 2002) has this term as: '1. prison. 2. coffer 3. sink or sewer in a byre.' Here it is used to define the space enclosed by the peat bank and its two ends

cas, the leg or handle of the *tairsgeir*

ceap, the large turf cut from the top of the peat bank and placed on the ground as a dry platform for the peat cutter

Ciamar a tha thu? How are you?

Ciamar a tha thu fhèin? How's yourself?

cianalas, homesickness, but more profoundly a longing for home

*corrad (cor-fàd), the outermost peat in the *barrad,* usually waste as it is the peat that is most exposed to the elements after each year's cutting

cro, the heel of the *tairsgeir*

cruach / beul na cruaich, the peat stack / open mouth or end of the peat stack

fàd a' chaorain, the bottom layer(s) of peat in the bank, that produce *mòine dhubh*

fàd a' ghàrraid, the second layer of peats in the bank, so called because in some regions they were used to build a wall of peats on top of the bank (near to its edge) that enabled drying and was also useful for banks that had insufficient dry ground surrounding the bank for the peats to be thrown flat for drying

fàd tasgaidh an teine, a peat used to smoulder a fire overnight. See *proghan*

Fàg Mi! Leave me!

Fàilte! Welcome!

faobhar, the cutting edge of the *tairsgeir* blade

feannagan, runrigs or lazy beds – raised areas of ground in straight rows used for growing potatoes in areas of thin soil cover

Fear na Slèibhtean, man of the mountains

fir-chlis, the Northern Lights or Aurora Borealis

*gaoth-talamh, literally 'wind ground'. This is an obscure, even rare term, which describes gashes in the face of the peat bank that come as a result of shrinkage and drying by the wind. See *snaidheadh*

gille Brighde, oystercatcher. In the introduction (p.14) to her book *Folksongs and Folklore of South Uist* (Routledge & Kegan Paul Ltd, London 1955), Margaret Fay Shaw writes: 'The first of February is St Bride's Day. In Gaelic tradition she was the foster-mother of Christ, and her name is in many ancient prayers. The oystercatcher, the black-and-white shore bird with scarlet legs and beak, is said to be her servant and is called in Gaelic *gille Brighde* or servant of Bride. The story is told that he once concealed Christ from his enemies by covering Him with seaweed and for that service he wears a cross on his back. The sea water is said to become warm on her day.'

laigh sios, lie down

*làrach isein, this term is perhaps one of the most obscure and local of terms the author has gathered. It refers to the space left by the peat cutter between the top of the peat bank and the first thrown or stacked peat in the wall; it literally means the space, or footprint of a small bird, or the space that a small bird would need to walk between the edge of the bank and the nearest peat

mallachadh, a curse or oath

marbh-phaisg, death shroud

mòine bhan, spongy 'white' or fibrous peat, often thick with grass considered excellent as *fàd tasgaidh a' teinne* and also *proghan*

mòine chruaidh ghlas, hard grey peat, similar to *mòine dhubh* in that it is very quick to dry. It often comes from banks containing loose boulders and stones. This type of peat is highly desirable, as it does not crumble or burn as rapidly as the *mòine dhubh*

mòine dhubh, hard black peat most often found at the very base of the peat bank, free from any solid organic matter.

na h-ailean, socket at the top of the *tairsgeir* blade into which the *cro* or handle is placed

naosg, snipe

neònach, unusual or strange (of a person)

procaid, whispered or secret speech

*proghan, *Dwelly's Illustrated Gaelic to English Dictionary* has the following definition: '1. dregs, lees, sediment, refuse. 2. mixture of the remains of different foods used to feed calves.' However, here its meaning is a large peat soaked in water that would be placed at the back of the fire at night to keep the fire burning slowly. This usage of this word was only familiar to the peat cutters encountered by the author in Ness. See also *fàd tasgaidh an teinne*

riachadh, scratch / scratching in peat cutting to mark out the surface area of the peat bank to be cut, often done with a spade

Rubha, the Point district of the Isle of Lewis

rudhan / rudhan beag, a small mound or dolmen-like stack of peats made by leaning three or four 'lifted' peats together when they have partially dried to enable further drying

rùisg, shave, make bare; in peat cutting to remove the top layer of turf from the bank to reveal the peat beneath

Salm, psalm

sgian, blade of the *tairsgeir*

sgoth / sgothan, traditional Lewis fishing boat(s)

Slàinte mhath! Good health!

Smeachan, the foot step on the *cro* or handle of the *tairsgeir*

*snaidheadh, *Dwelly's Illustrated Gaelic to English Dictionary* defines this term as follows: '1. hewing, act of hewing down, or reducing to form by hewing. 2. whetting, act of whetting or sharpening. 3. consuming, act of consuming. 4. blocking 5. defalcating. 6. slicing, lopping. 7. pining away. 8. carving. 9. carving. [. . .] It is used here to describe the act of smoothing the face of the peat bank after cutting to ensure that it is weather-resistant. Any small cuts or gashes in the face will be dried and opened by the wind, hence ruining part of the peat bank for next year's cutting. Great pride is taking in getting a fine finish on the banks after cutting. Term gathered on 'field trip' in Ness, as described above. See also *gaoth-talamh*

taghairm, Dwelly's Illustrated Gaelic to English Dictionary defines this word as follows: '1.echo. 2. gathering summons. 3. ancient means of diviniation, said to be one of the most effectual ways of raising the devil, and getting unlawful wishes gratified. The performance consisted in roasting cats alive, one after the other, for some days without tasting food; which if duly persisted in, summoned a legion of devils, in the guide of black cats, with their master at their head, all screeching in a way terrifying to any person of ordinary nerves. – NGP. The diviniation by the t. was once a noted superstition among the Gwel, and in the northern parts of the Lowlands of Scotland. When any important question concerning futurity arose, and of which a solution was, by all means, desirable, some shrewder person than his neighbours was pitched upon, to perform the part of a prophet. The person was wrapped in the warm smoking hide of a newly slain ox or cow, commonly an ox, and laid at full length in the wildest recess of some lonely waterfall. The question was then out to him, and the oracle was left in solitude to consider it. Here he lay for some hours with his cloak of knowledge around him, and over his head, no doubt, to see better into futurity; deafened by the incessant roaring of the torrent; every sense assailed; his body steaming; his fancy in ferment; and whatever notion had found its way into his mind from so mnay sources of prophecy, it was firmly believed to have been communicated by invisible beings who were supposed to haunt such solitudes . . .'

In this description, Dwelly and his advisors provide a vital link to the myth and spiritual culture of the Gael from its pre-Christian origins. The description enables the suggestion that there are clear links between the Gael and other shamanic cultures and practices found in other Arctic and sub-Arctic regions

tairsgeir, the long handled implement with a right angled blade used to cut peat

Tha gu math, I'm very good/well

Tha mi alright, I'm alright

Thig a-staigh! Come in!

---

*The author gathered these terms and descriptions from peat cutters at banks east of Ness in the Isle of Lewis, in the summer of 2001, during a field trip collecting old Gaelic words associated with the peats, and in subsequent conversations with peat cutters from Ness and Back.

Songs

Is a Dia fèin a's buacheil dhomh
The Lord's Prayer, Psalm 23

Cumha Mhic An-Toisich (Macintosh's Lament)
Full lyrics as follows:

> *Ochòin a laoigh, leag iad thu,*
> *Leag iad thu, laoigh, leag iad thu*
> *Ochòin a laoigh, leag iad thu,*
> *'M bealach a'ghàrraidh.*
>
> *'S truagh nach robh mis' an sin* (3x)
> *'S ceathr' air gach làimh dhomh.*
>
> *An leann thog iad gu d'bhanais* (3x)
> *Air d'fhalairidh bha e.*
>
> *Bha mi 'm bhréidich am ghruagaich* (3x)
> *'S am bhanntraich 's an aon uair ud.*
>
> *Gun chron air an t-saoghal ort* (3x)
> *Ach nach d'fheud thu saoghal buan fhàistinn.*

This song is as performed by Margaret Stewart (vocals) and Allan MacDonald (bagpipes – Sinclair chanter), on their CD *Fhuair Mi Pog* (CDTRAX 132). Allan MacDonald provides a full note on this most ancient of pibrochs in the sleevenote to the CD. This song is notoriously difficult to translate into English and at the same time to retain all of its poignant beauty. Therefore, here are two translations, the first by Margaret Stewart, and the second by Morag Macleod.

> *(Chorus:)*
> Alas my love they knocked you down,
> Knocked you down, my love, knocked you down,

Alas my love they knocked you down,
In the mire of the enclosure.

(Verse:)

Pity that I was not there,
Pity that I was not there
Pity that I was not there
With four others each side of me

(Chorus)

(Verse:)

The ale they took to your wedding,
The ale they took to your wedding,
The ale they took to your wedding,
Was drunk at your wake.

(Chorus)

(Verse:)
I was a virgin then a married woman
I was a virgin then a married woman
I was a virgin then a married woman
And then a widow in the space of one day

(Chorus)

(Verse:)
You were faultless in this world,
You were faultless in this world,
You were faultless in this world,
only that you were unable to predict/promise
a long life for us together

(Chorus)

The following is the version from Morag Macleod:

Alas, my darling, they laid you down,
Alas, my darling, they laid you down in the gap of the dyke.

What a pity I was not there (2x)
With four supporters on either side of me.

The ale they got for your wedding feast (2x)
Was at your wake instead.

I was a bride, a maid (2x)
And a widow at that one stroke.

With not a fault in the world in you (2x)
Except that a long life was not allowed for you.

An Till Mise Chaoidh (Will I Ever Return?)
The lyrics to this most beautiful of Gaelic songs are as follows:

An till mise chaoidh dha na glinn sa robh mi òg,
Far 'm bu chridheil aoibhneach sinn gun uallach inntinn oirnn
A bhuachailleachd chrodh-laoigh agus ghaimhne mar bu nòs
An duil an till mi chaoidh dha na glinn sa robh mo òg.

Gur tric a bhios mi cuimhneachadh gach loch is beinn is òb,
Smeòrach ghlas nan glinn seinn gu binn a-measg nan còs
An crodh is iad cho riaraichte, air lèaintean 'g ith an fheòir
'S a' ghrian is i dol sìos 'n taobh a-siar do Locha Ròg.

Cha leig mis' air dhìochuimhn am feasgar fèathach reòidht'
An eala bhàn a' sgiamhail 's i sgiathalaich m' an òb
A' ghealach cho ion-mhiannaichte a' riaghladh anns na neòil,
Is fuaim tràigh Uig is Shanndabhaig – O, b'annsa leam an ceòl.

'S ged is fhada thall tha mi gun ghanntas ne mo stòr,
Mo dhùrachd bhith measg bheanntan is ghleanntan Eilein Leòdh's

Tha dùil agam bhith ann m'an tig feasgar fann mo lò,
Is luthaiginn bhith air m'adhlacadh aig ceann traigh Dhaile Mòir.

(A' cheud rann a-rithist)

This song was written by Calum MacLeòid of Geàrrannan, on the west side of the Isle of Lewis, in 1925, at a time when Calum was living in Detroit. Here, the song is as sung by Seonag Niccoinnich (Joan MacKenzie) and is from her CD *Seonag Niccoinnich*, number 19 in the Scottish Tradition series of the School of Scottish Studies, University of Edinburgh (CDTRAX 9019).

The song is a lament sung by one, like its author, who is away from the Island, thinking of his home and the birds and wildlife around the loch (Loch Ròg), and wondering if he will ever return to the land he longs for. In fact, Calum MacLeòid did return home and is buried in the cemetery at Dalmore. The English translation of this song is by Margaret Stewart.

Will I ever return to the glens where I was young?
Where we were cheerful and happy without a care in the world,
Herding the cattle and calves as was our tradition;
I wonder if I will ever go back to the glen where I was young?

I often think of each loch, hill and pool,
The grey mavis of the glens singing sweetly in the hollows.
The cattle, so contentedly grazing on the meadows
And the sun going down to the west of Loch Roag

I will not forget the calm frosty evenings,
The white swan calling as she flew around the bay.
The moon so captivating, dominating the heavens
And the sound of Uig Sands and Sanndabhaig – oh how I long for
    their music.

Although I may be far away and wanting for nothing,
My wish is to be amongst the hills and glens of the island of Lewis.
I hope to return there before my days come to an end,
And my wish is to be laid to rest by the sands of Daile Mòr.

Acknowledgements and thanks

The author wishes to thank: publisher Polygon and editors Marion Sinclair and Alison Rae; Greentrax Recordings for permission to reproduce the lyrics of 'Cumha Mhic An-Toisich' (Macintosh's Lament) and 'An Till Mise Chaoidh' (both recordings and texts are copyright Greentrax Recordings); Tom Lowenstein for permission to use his translation of Uvavnuk's poem 'Moved'; Angela Morrison, Lews Castle College, for her help and patience with my Gaelic and the glossary; Margaret Stewart and Morag Macleod for advice and for the fine English language translations of the Gaelic songs – both translations are copyright these authors; Iain Norman and Pauline Morrison, Ness and the peat cutters of Ness for some fine old Gaelic words; Steve Dilworth for advice on whale dentistry; Norman and Christine Martin; Anne and Tom Ramsay, and all my friends in Back for their support and encouragement; Chrissie Bel for her support, love of the Gaelic and the island of Lewis; Giles Gordon for encouragement; and the Scottish Arts Council for the New Writers Bursary. Finally, many people have inspired, helped and advised me in the making of this novel. Any mistakes and inaccuracies are mine alone, especially the Gaelic.